FOREVER FAITHFUL

Leana
Thanks for the support
Great to meet you at GCU
2017 ♡
Happy Reading
I Sabella
2017

FOREVER FAITHFUL

ISABELLA

SAPPHIRE BOOKS

SALINAS, CALIFORNIA

Forever Faithful
Copyright © 2014 by **Isabella** All rights reserved.

ISBN - 978-1-939062-75-8

This is a work of fiction - names, characters, places, and incidents are the product of the author's imagination or are used fictitiously. Any resemblance to actual persons living or dead, business, events, or locales is entirely coincidental. The combat situations in this book are fictional and any resemblance to actual events is entirely coincidental.

All rights reserved. No part of this publication may be reproduced, distributed, or transmitted in any form or by any means, including photocopying, recording, or other electronic or mechanical methods, without written permission of the publisher.

Editor - Kaycee Hawn
Book Designer- LJ Reynolds
Cover Design- Christine Svendsen

Sapphire Books
Salinas, CA 93912
www.sapphirebooks.com

Printed in the United States of America
First edition – February 2015

This and other Sapphire Books titles can be found at
www.sapphirebooks.com

Dedication

To the SPC 4 who started all this, you give me more than I will ever be able to give back. I am forever faithful, to you.

To my sons. My life is forever better for having you in it.

Acknowledgments

They say it takes a village, well in this case it took the help of some wonderful women and men in the military to take this book somewhere I've never been, combat. A big thanks to AJ Johnson for her candid responses to my questions. I couldn't have had Afghanistan as a back drop without her help. To Rachel R, who doesn't know it, but without her detailed telling of her job in Afghanistan, this book wouldn't be what it is now. And to Erin for questioning everything, hugs to you and Kim.

To the readers! I appreciate all of your support, feedback, and encouragement. I love when I can meet you, talk to you, and just hang out.

To my Sapphire sisters. You ladies rock! You inspire me with all you do.

LK, what can I say, you have taught me so much, but then you probably hear that a lot. Thanks for your guidance, friendship, and counsel. You're a gem!

Chapter One

As Nic stepped out and around the Humvee, a metal click barely pierced her consciousness. It suddenly registered, and she knew it signaled danger. The air around her vibrated as the explosion launched her and anything in her vicinity backwards.

"Bom—," was all she could squeeze out before she tasted dirt in her mouth.

The sun had been eclipsed, darkness engulfed her, and she struggled to take a breath.

Blackness.

Silence.

Claire.

Grace.

The smell of Jasmine filled the warm air. She loved Jasmine; it reminded her of Claire. Momentary thoughts flashed through her mind. She saw Claire standing in front of her, beautiful in her white dress, a wedding dress, clutching a small bouquet of wild flowers. Grace stood next to her mom; a soft light blue dress rustled as she danced around her mom's legs, laughing. Nic smiled and bent down to pick Grace up, swinging her around, and around, and around, until Nic was dizzy.

"More, Nickie," Grace said, laughing, her arms stretched out. Suddenly Grace was slipping from her grip, falling away from Nic. The harder Nic tried to hold on to Grace, the faster she moved away, slipping further into the darkness.

"Grace," Nic said, reaching for her daughter. Fingertips touched and then Grace was gone.

Nic glanced around her, but she couldn't see anything in the pitch black. It was surreal. One minute she's swinging Grace, the next she was standing alone. Her body felt like it was on fire, coupled with the distinct smell of something burning. Nic turned to her right. The sergeant standing next to her was on fire.

"Sergeant, you're burning."

"Ma'am?"

"Sergeant, look," Nic pointed to the sergeant's arms. "Fire."

Blackness again.

"Nic, honey?"

Claire stood over Nic, smiling down at her.

"What are you doing here, baby?" Nic touched Claire's face. Her bloody fingers left a trail down the delicate pink skin of Claire's neck. Turning her hands over, Nic saw the skin was broken, bleeding, and charred. The coppery smell assaulted her as she tried to wipe the blood off of Claire's face. "I'm sorry, sweetheart." The smudges only grew as she pushed her broken fingers across Claire's skin and down her white dress.

"Colonel..." Nic's body shook. Nic strained to see something, anything, but there was barely any light coming into the tunnel she found herself in. She thought she heard something, but now she wasn't so sure.

"Colonel...open your eyes, Ma'am."

There is was again, a noise just out of earshot. She tried to move, but lead had replaced her muscles, keeping her pinned down. Each breath was taxing in the effort it took just to inhale; opening her mouth to gulp down more air, she choked on the dirt that coated her mouth. The distinct smell of cordite, blood, and smoke filled her lungs each time she barely inhaled. Again, the taste of blood and dirt mixed with the small pebbles in her mouth. Trying to spit, she tried to clear her throat, but could barely move her jaw. Pain jagged through her head the harder she tried to open her mouth

"*Fuck.*"

She wasn't dead.

"Ma'am?" The voice sounded like it was calling down to her from somewhere far above her.

Where the fuck was she and how the hell did she get here?

Darkness enveloped her and she faded back into the abyss she'd just been swimming around in.

Chapter Two

2 months before the explosion

"Congrats, Colonel Caldwell, you're being sent to Afghanistan."

"Excuse me?" Nic felt like the floor had just fallen out from under her. Suddenly her head was swimming. Surely he hadn't just said she was being shipped out overseas, not to Afghanistan. "Is this some kind of joke?"

"I don't joke, Colonel Caldwell," the provost said, then thumbed through a file and spread it across his desk. "Your mentor has recommended you for the assignment. It's a new position the defense department has put together. There is a civilian going over there to interview tribal elders, connect with them, and find out how they interact with the Taliban. Besides, you owe the Marine Corps a payback tour and yours is Afghanistan."

"Sir, I was told that I would be doing research here at the Naval Postgraduate School as my payback tour. There must be some mistake."

He rolled a fat cigar between his thick lips, wetting the outside and then biting the end. There was no smoking inside the building, but she suspected there wasn't anyone around that outranked the arrogant bastard.

Nic had never meshed with her mentor. After

arriving at the Naval Postgraduate School, she'd reported for duty and changed her degree from engineering to counter-terrorism, which put her smack dab in the middle of his program. From what she'd heard, she was the first woman in his program and he'd made it clear that he didn't think women were cut out for the counter-terrorism focus of the degree. He'd made it extremely tough for her to pass his two classes. He constantly encouraged the men, while he ignored her raised hand, and at the end, she just blurted out answers. Finally she'd just given up trying and was happy to pass the damn classes. This was the last semester of her education, so passing was the most important thing to her; ranking mattered in the beginning, but now screw it and him. Clearly, she wouldn't be at the top of her class, no thanks to that bastard.

She'd seen the provost of the school and her mentor laughing it up in the Poseidon room at the Officer's club. In fact, she'd made it a point to go over and greet her advisor, just to try and get an introduction to the commandant.

Big mistake.

"Good afternoon, sir,"

"Colonel Caldwell, shouldn't you be at the library studying for your next exam?" he said smugly.

"Just came from there. I thought I'd grab a bite to eat and then hit the books again. Sir," she said, offering her hand to the commandant. "Colonel Nichole Caldwell. How are you?"

"Colonel," he said; a hint of distain laced his next words. "I understand from your advisor you'd like a research position here?"

"Yes, sir."

"Hmm."

"She's the only female in the class," her advisor offered.

"Really. Seen combat?"

"Sir?"

"Have you done a combat tour, yet?" The commandant picked up his beer and leaned his massive frame against the bar.

It was the way he emphasized 'yet' that bothered her. She wasn't about to recite her whole military record, just to suck up. Lay out her time overseas. She'd seen plenty who recited it like a mantra every chance they had. That wasn't her.

"Yes sir, Iraq."

"Hmm. In my day we didn't see women on the ship, hell, we didn't even see 'em till we got shore leave and then they were only…" He looked up at Nic, who must have had a disapproving look on her face, because he stopped and sipped his beer. "Well, I guess things are different now, aren't they?"

It had gone all downhill after that. She finally excused herself; she clearly wasn't part of this old boys club. What had she been thinking?

His smug smile irked her as he continued to talk around the cigar. "You *are* doing research, Colonel. You'll be working out of Camp Leatherneck in the Helmand Province in Afghanistan. You and some civilian are being sent over to interview the local tribes. Seems the government wants you to interact with the natives and gather information for research being done by some governmental agency. They want to learn about the locals and how they interact with the Taliban, or some bullshit like that," he said dismissively. "I'd just bomb the shit out of 'em if it was me, but this ain't my war."

No, this wasn't his war; hell, it wasn't Nic's either. She'd paid her dues and now she couldn't believe that the Corps was sending her overseas, again. How was she going to tell Claire? What about Grace? She'd grown up a lot in the three years they'd been in Monterey and now she was a little cuddle bug Nic couldn't live without.

Nic stared down at the orders in her hand. She still couldn't wrap her mind around what she was being told.

"I'm reserve, sir. I have a family," she said, barely realizing she'd given her thoughts voice.

"You're a Marine, Colonel Caldwell."

The man staring back at her was right out of a forties movie. His starched uniform, flat top, and grizzled exterior made her think of John Wayne. He was from another time and his next words proved it.

"Colonel Caldwell, if the Marines wanted you to have a family they would have issued you one. You feelin' me?"

"Sir?" *What an asshole*, she thought as she fingered the silver oak leaf on her cover.

"I know things are different for you LBGT in the military. You get the same benefits as those who live by God's law and I have to accommodate you and your girlfriend the same way as all the other wives, but it doesn't mean I gotta like it."

"No sir, I don't suppose it does," Nic said, her voice peppered with sarcasm. "But you *will* respect the rank. I've earned that much."

DOMA might have been repealed, but it was the same military ten minutes after the decision that it was ten minutes before the decision. The fact that the Commandant of the Marine Corps had come out against the repeal practically gave carte blanche to anyone who wanted to keep those same bullshit views they had when women and blacks wanted to integrate into the military. She wasn't surprised this old bastard was holding on with a death grip to his hate-filled views. A year later, it was pretty much the same. Some command structures would never change in the Navy and Marine Corps. They had a long history of being deep in male attitude. Shit, she'd seen women who she swore had grown a set of testicles just to stay on a commander's good side. She was only sorry she couldn't make the provost eat his words.

Standing, she squeezed her orders, the paper crinkling in her hand, and said, "Will that be all, sir?"

"You deploy with the rest of the team after your graduation."

"I don't get a few days between school and deployment?"

"Yep, you'll get about a month to get your records ready, shots, and all your paperwork in order and then you're overseas. I suggest you get things squared away, Colonel."

The muscles in his jaw bunched as he started to grind his teeth. Orders weren't meant to be questioned, just followed – to the letter.

"Thank you for the advice, sir. Permission to leave, sir."

The provost leaned back in his chair and made a point of giving her a once over before he went back to the paperwork littering his desk, ignoring her completely.

She stood ramrod straight and waited, crumbling the paperwork more as she clenched her fist tighter. He might like jerking her chain, but she was still a Marine and she wasn't about to dishonor the Corps. Another minute passed before he finally said something.

"Dismissed."

His disrespect to her rank pissed her off. He didn't have to like her as a person, but she'd earned her rank and his bullshit move and his flagrant disrespectful statements grated on her with each step she took towards the door. She wished she could take it up with the IG, but she wanted the research job and she'd promised Claire they'd stay in Monterey and build a life for themselves. Taking on this jerk would sever that chance, for good. She grabbed the handle, but stopped and turned to go back to the asshat's office just as her phone went off.

Karma, she thought, looking down at the photo splashed across the screen. Someone wasn't going to allow her to throw her career away, just to make a point.

Claire.

"Hey baby, what's up?" Nic smiled. A call from Claire was the highlight of many a stressful day. She couldn't help but relax at hearing Claire's cheerful voice.

"Hi Honey, just wondering when you'll be home for lunch."

It was their Wednesday ritual since she started back to school. Most of her days were spent in the library doing research, but Wednesdays were special. Their time for planning their lives, to talk about Grace, or just sit in the back yard and hold hands. It was sappy, but it was her and Claire's most intimate time outside the bedroom.

Nic twisted her watch. "About ten minutes."

"You okay?"

Claire knew her well enough that she couldn't lie to her, but news like this had to be told face-to-face. God, how was she going to tell Claire she was being deployed? Nic always knew it was a possibility. When you went to college on the military dime, you owed them. She'd figured since she'd been wounded in action in Iraq, she'd stay closer to home. In fact, she'd applied to work in research at NPS and all signs were a go for a research position, but the military always made other plans and rarely did they ever fit yours.

"Nic?"

"Huh? Yeah, I'm good, I'll be home in a few. I love you."

"I love you too, baby."

Shit, shit, shit. Nic positioned her cap and pushed the door wide, slamming it against the cinderblock building. Her uniform suddenly felt like a straightjacket she wasn't about to get out of anytime soon.

Chapter Three

Claire bit the inside of her lip. Something was wrong with Nic and she knew it, she felt it. Nic's voice was distant and strained. Maybe graduation was weighing on her. Claire had taken the liberty of putting together a party for this milestone in Nic's life. It surprised both of them when Nic's parents said they'd come. Maybe Nic's dad had mellowed with age. It happened. She, on the other hand, had passed on inviting her dad. He was a sore spot in her life and she wasn't feeling contrite enough to endure his fire and brimstone attitude. Jordan would be there and a few fellows from Nic's class were coming.

Nic had plans for her life and they'd made a decision to live off post in the event they stayed in the area. That was if she got the research job. Nic had switched her major to some sort of counter-terrorism degree, adding an extra semester, but it seemed to be a better fit; at least, that's what Nic told her. Nic explained that the job opportunities were endless with the new degree. Once Nic was done, she'd promised Claire it was her turn to go back to college. Now Claire had to decide what her future would look like. The local university, California State Monterey Bay, had a few programs that looked interesting, assuming they stayed.

"Mommy, mommy, come 'er."

Grace ran through the house, hand trailing

behind her, reaching for her mother.

"Grace, no running through the house."

It was a constant reprimand. She wished she could just put on a recording and push play every time Grace raced around. Grace was growing up to be a dynamo that never seemed to run out of energy, but the minute her head hit the pillow, she was down for the count. Amazing.

"It's time for your nap, young lady," Claire reminded, following behind her daughter. The last three years had seen Grace flower into a slightly more mature little girl with a tomboy attitude. Nic attributed it to all the boys living in housing. Without other little girls to play dolls with, Grace was socialized just like the boys. Gone were the dolls in her toy box, replaced with toy helicopters, cars, and, much to Claire's dismay, a few toy guns. Mostly of the water variety, but Nic had convinced her that if they made them taboo, Grace would covet them and since most of her playgroup was comprised of boys, Clare suspected Nic was right. She'd thrown a doll or two into the toy box on the off chance Grace would find her softer, gentler side.

Claire had been momentarily thrilled to see Grace playing with her dolls today, until she realized Grace was using her makeup to turn them into zombies.

"Zombies?" Claire said, still shocked at the answer. "Where did you hear about zombies?"

"Tim's house. His parents let him watch 'em on T.V."

Grace blacked out an eye with eyeliner and then added smudges on the doll's arms and legs. "This is where her skin is falling off, and look, mommy, she's missing an eye. I poked it out." Grace shoved the doll in Claire's face.

It's just a phase, Claire chanted under her breath. She would be talking to Tim's mom at the next playgroup meeting.

"They eat people you know," she said so matter-of-factly.

"They aren't real, Grace."

"Yes, they are, and Tim says we have to get ready for the apolips, mommy."

Claire picked up Grace and turned her towards her. "No more Tim's house until I speak to his mother."

"Mommy," Grace said, throwing herself backwards, almost toppling them both to the floor.

"Nap time, honey."

"Mommy…I'm not tired."

"Yes, I know."

When will she grow out of this stage? Claire wondered. *Careful what you wish for,* she could hear Nic say. *Pretty soon she'll be in prom dresses and boys and then what?*

Claire leaned against the doorframe and watched Grace push a doll up her arm. Grace was losing the fight to stay awake, drowsy eyes and a pouty mouth signs she was giving up the ghost, so to speak.

Claire sat on the bed, cradling her daughter close. What would she do when she was chasing boys for all the wrong reasons? Trying to banish the thought from her mind, she clutched Grace closer, laying her head on her chest. She felt Grace relax against her, the fight gone.

"Mommy?"

"Hmm?"

"Why do I have two mommies and Tim only has one?"

Aw, the looming realization that her parents were different. She knew it was coming, but Claire didn't expect it quite yet.

"Cause you're lucky."

God, what a stupid answer, she thought, pulling Grace closer. Gently she laid Grace down on the bed and lay beside her, threading her fingers through sweaty hair, pushing the unruly mess out of Grace's face.

"Can we find Tim another mom?"

"What?" She had to stop herself from giggling at the notion that Tim needed another mom. What would Tim's dad say?

"Yeah, he needs another mom, too."

"It's not that easy honey."

"But you have Nic and you love each other, so Tim's mom needs another mommy to love her, too."

Oh, the innocence of youth. If life were only that simple.

"Grace, honey, it's different for me and Nic. We like each other and Tim's mom likes boys. So I don't think she would want another mommy."

"Why?"

The doll was pushed up her shoulder, her neck and then Grace pointed the doll's face at Claire and waited for a kiss. Complying with the silent request gave Claire a moment to try and make sense of something that most adults didn't understand. What makes a woman love another woman? She could go clinical but Grace wouldn't understand, she could say it was just nature, but she wasn't quite sure Grace would get that either.

She'd told herself she would treat it as a normal relationship, but society, parents, and kids will fill

Grace's head with other ideas if she didn't treat it with the respect it deserved. They weren't any more different than any other couple. She and Nic went shopping, paid bills, and looked at having a mortgage in the near future, and were a committed couple just like everyone else. The only difference was they were two women.

"Mommy?" A sleep-laden voice beckoned.

"Yes, sweetie?"

"When are you and Nic going to get a wedding?"

"You mean married?"

"Uh huh."

"Oh, I don't know, why?"

Marriage.

She and Nic hadn't talked about it in a while, but now that DOMA was a thing of the past, there wasn't any reason why they couldn't. Assuming Nic wanted to get married. It would give them more benefits, but that wasn't a reason to get married. They'd celebrated the repeal of DOMA, reminded each other that they could get married, legally, and promised each other that after graduation they would seal the deal. Even if it was just a justice of the peace sort of thing. A grand party wasn't needed, but Nic had reminded Claire she'd never been married, so maybe a small ceremony was in order, especially for Grace. The message they sent to their daughter about marriage would stick with her for the rest of her life. Nic always worried about Grace and it warmed Claire's heart every time she put Grace's comfort before Nic's. A true parent without the biology.

"Tim says you can't get married 'cause you eat carpet." Grace turned over and faced the wall. Everything said so innocently that a six year old didn't realize what she was saying. "I told him you don't eat carpet. Do you?"

That little bastard, Claire thought. Her temper flared. She was going to have to have a talk with Tim's mother. Bitch. Before she could say anything, soft snores were floating from Grace.

It had finally happened. Grace was old enough to ask questions, have her opinions formed by others, and hear the disgusting comments usually only said by adults. Grace didn't know she was different or that her parents were different. The world just encroached on Grace's perfect little world with just a few ill-spoken words from a playmate.

Carpet muncher, marriage, what else would today bring?

Chapter Four

Nic reached around Claire and snagged a tomato and popped it in her mouth, but not before Claire swatted her hand.

"Where's Grace?"

"Taking a nap. She doesn't like salad, so I thought we'd eat lunch while she's down for the count."

"I like salad," Nic said, smiling and kissing Claire's ear and down her neck. "In fact, I'd like to toss your salad." Nic took the knife from Clair's hands and turned her around, and pulled Claire close. "Hmm, you smell good."

"You say that every time I cook." Claire giggled.

"No, I say that every time I'm near you." Nic's lips moved close to Claire's lips, close enough to feel her warm breath. Spearmint, Claire always smelled of her favorite mint.

Nic's hands slid down against the soft swell of Claire's hips and behind her, pushing her hips against Nic's. Swaying against Claire, Nic whispered in her ear. "Up."

Claire smiled, letting her gaze roam over Nic's sexy uniform. It was one of the few days Nic had to report to work in her dress uniform and Claire almost melted when she caught sight of Nic in it that morning. She purred as she slinked across the bed towards Nic.

"Colonel, you look…"

"Dashing?"

"Hmm, not the word I was thinking of," she said, running a finger across the ribbons on Nic's chest. "Hot, sexy, commanding...."

"Commanding, really." Nic smirked as she held Claire tighter.

"Edible," Claire whispered in Nic's ear.

Claire wrapped her arms around Nic's neck as Nic easily lifted Claire off her feet and wrapped her legs around Nic. Now they were eye level and smiling at each other. She never got enough of Claire and lately they'd rarely found time to be alone, with Grace running around under foot. So Nic took advantage of every opportune moment to seduce her girlfriend.

Pushing through the patio door, Nic's devious smile conveyed her intentions. Pulling a sheet off the line, she tossed it on the lawn and kneeled down, Claire resting on her thighs.

"Hey, that's clean wash."

"I know and we have a perfectly good dryer. So, I don't know why you want to hang it out, but I'm glad you did," she said, as she put Claire gently on the sheet. Framing Claire with her hands, Nic stared down at her, wishing she could make this moment last forever. Time was always fleeting for them. Playgroups, PTA, school, meetings, and now the possibility of a deployment to Afghanistan weighed on Nic.

"I like the way it smells when I make the bed. Besides, I'm going–" Nic lowered her lips, capturing Claire in mid-sentence. Soon, Grace would be up and Nic had an urgency about her that she couldn't explain. She needed Claire; she needed Claire to open herself to Nic, to want her as much as she wanted Claire. Parting Claire's lips with her tongue, she pushed through until she could taste mint. They dueled for domination, but

Claire relaxed into the kiss.

Claire tugged on Nic's shirt hem.

"Hmm."

"Off," Claire said, struggling to untuck the uniform top from her slacks.

Leaning up, Nic unbuttoned a few buttons and lifted her arms as Claire peeled it up and off. "We might be seen back here."

"Not likely, our neighbors are quite a ways away. Besides, you never worry when we're in the Jacuzzi."

"Yeah, but it's dark when we're in there."

Nic couldn't help herself as she pushed herself further between Claire's legs, her pubic bone resting against Claire's. She slowly started to move her hips suggestively against Claire's as her tongue glided along Claire's jaw, and her hands slipped under Claire's shirt. Palming her breasts, Nic let her thumb and finger pinch at the taunt nipples underneath before she slipped her hand under the lace cups.

"What would the neighbors say if they could see us?"

"I'm thinking George would just sit and watch. I'm sure we've blown every lesbian porno he's watched or going to watch. Besides, if the neighbors are creeepin' then they get what they deserve, a hard on," Nic said, pulling the bra and tank off Claire.

"You're so bad."

"Yeah, but I'm so good at it."

"Yes, you are."

Nic could feel Claire's smile against her cheek as she rubbed her face against Claire's. Closing her eyes, she memorized this moment—the closeness, Claire's scent, her soft, silky skin under her fingers. Everything about Claire sent Nic's heart into overdrive lately.

Sometimes she would sit and watch Claire sleep, wishing she could reach out and touch her lover, satisfied with tracing the lines of her sexy body.

"Up," Nic commanded. Claire lifted her hips as Nic slid Claire's shorts off.

"Commando?"

"I was in a hurry to get Grace off to bed and lunch started."

"Lucky me."

Nic twirled her finger and Claire flipped over, exposing her soft round ass to Nic. "God, I love this view."

"Again, shall I remind you of the neighbor–"

A resounding swat on Claire's ass made her flinch and start to giggle.

"Shh." Nic lowered herself on to Claire, weaved her arms under Claire's, and threaded their fingers together, resting on her elbows. She didn't want all of her weight on Claire, just enough to dominate her, so to speak. Nic started to press against Claire's ass, her hips gently grinding just enough to stimulate them both.

Lowering her lips to Claire's ear, she whispered, "You make me crazy, you know that?"

"Crazy is as crazy does." Claire turned her head and tried to kiss Nic, but she pulled back.

"Really?"

"Hmm." Claire closed her eyes and bit her lower lip seductively. "You look so hot in that uniform, Colonel. My body squeals every time I see you in it."

Still working her hips against Claire's ass, Nic raised up, letting Claire's hands go and waiting for Claire to turn over. They'd done this dance a hundred times and Nic never tired of it. The back and forth dance of lovers. That quickening that happened when her lover pulled her heartstrings. Leaning off to the side, Nic rested her head on her outstretched arm and traced a mindless pattern across Claire's stomach, watching it contract as she moved her finger closer to a breast.

"You know what makes me hot?"

Claire shook her head. Baiting Nic, she took Nic's finger and slid it into her mouth. Her tongue flicked across the tip. She added another of Nic's fingers, wetting them both and then painting them across her nipple.

"This?" Claire said, wetting the tips again and rubbing them across the other nipple.

"God, you're good at this." Nic pulled Claire in tighter and slung a leg over her hips. Her naked breasts pressed against Claire's.

"You have too many clothes on, lover," Claire whispered.

"Do I?"

Nic felt Claire work the buckle on her belt, slipping her pants open and press her palm against her, sliding further into her briefs. Before she could say anything, Claire was fingering her.

Chapter Five

"Let's get married." Nic wound a strand of Claire's hair back and forth between her fingers. The afterglow of sex permeated her body and clouded her mind, and she wanted to keep this feeling forever, with Claire and only Claire. Afghanistan was forcing her to act quickly. Time wasn't her friend; shit, it was the same for every war, for every person leaving for a battle zone. Put a stamp on your loved one and leave knowing that there would be someone waiting for you when you got back. She didn't have that when she shipped out to Iraq. Now she had it and she didn't want to lose it, ever.

"What?"

"Let's get married. DOMA's gone. We don't have a reason *not* to tie the knot."

Nic pulled the sheet over their bodies as Claire snuggled closer. The briefest smell of sex mixed with laundry softener caught Nic's attention and took her back in time to a moment with her grandmother.

"Smells, Honey. Smells are what you'll remember about a moment in your life. When you smell it again it will take you back instantly to that one place and time you first smelled it," her grandmother said, placing a warm slice of brownie and a glass of milk in front of her.

If she could box this moment, this smell, and take it with her to Afghanistan, she would. With Claire in her arms, she forgot about the world, but it was never far from the edges of their lives, even here in Monterey, and now it pressed even closer. How was she going to tell Claire about her orders to Afghanistan?

"We need to talk, Nic." Claire buried herself deeper in Nic's embrace.

The way Claire said it put a chill down her spine. It wasn't the flowery way she said it when she wanted something. God, she loved when Claire plied her feminine wiles on her; she was good at it. This time it sounded different. Trying to think back over the past week, she wondered if she missed something. Something that might have been said, or an action that might have been overlooked. In her younger days, Nic had broken it off with a girlfriend after a wild night of sex. She'd pissed her off, created a fight, and then—bam, it was over. It'd been too easy and she'd been too young to care. Why she would think about that particular memory at this time surprised Nic. Break up? What was she thinking? Her mind was a jumble of thoughts because of her impending deployment and she didn't like not being focused.

Thinking about what some of the guys talked about when she'd first arrived at NPS came back to her. It was often said that those who attended NPS got one of the four D's—divorce, dependent, dog, or deployed. Nic's heart skipped a few beats. There was no way they had a dependent on the way, and the dog thing was on the back burner until Grace was older. Oh God, maybe she wanted out! Did Claire already know her news? Impossible.

"Okay." Nic couldn't hide the hesitation in her voice as she pushed Claire back to look at her. She'd just asked the woman of her dreams to marry her and there wasn't a happy dance following the question. Something wasn't quite right.

"Grace said some things to me today as I was putting her down for her nap."

The tension in Nic's body eked up slightly. Grace. "What did she say?" Nic couldn't imagine what a six-year-old would say that would require an intense conversation between them. Grace was the most well behaved, precocious kid in school. Okay, maybe she was biased, but Nic had seen the other kids and they were mean, even in Nic's eyes, and she'd seen a lot during her time in the military. Maybe it was a coping mechanism; never let anyone close 'cause they were only going to be a momentary blip in your life, but never the less—some kids were animals.

"She's finally decided she likes dolls?" Nic joked, trying to lighten the mood and remembering the dust-up she and Claire had about a couple of squirt guns she'd tossed in Grace's toy box. Nic had seen Grace chasing the boys, who had toy guns, while she made a pretend gun with her fingers, shooting at them. So it made sense to grab a couple at the store and give them to their daughter. Funny how she thought of Grace as her and Claire's daughter now. Mike was only a man, in a picture, in a photo album.

"Hmm, no, she asked when we were going to get married."

"She did, did she? What did you tell her?" Nic felt guilty now that she hadn't made it legal. She'd been too focused on school, graduation, and now she had to tell Claire she was being deployed. God, life sucked sometimes.

"I didn't really tell her anything, 'cause her question was followed by a statement that left me a little speechless." Claire rested her chin on Nic's chest and smiled.

"What did she say?"

"She said that her little friend Tim told her we couldn't because we were carpet munchers."

"He what?"

"Yep, we are now the official carpet munchers in the neighborhood."

"Oh, that is just disgusting. I think I need to go have a talk with Tim's mommy and daddy. I can't believe someone in the Navy talks like that in front of his children. Fucking bullshit." Nic tried to sit up, but Claire pushed against her chest, keeping her down.

"We are not going to do this pissed off. We're going to talk to Grace, and then we're going to go over to Tim's house and have a discussion with his parents."

"Yes dear." Nic pulled Claire on top of her and grabbed her ass. "Kiss me."

ഇഇഇഇ

"Sweetheart?" Nic doodled something on her back. The tip of her finger dipped between the cheeks of Claire's ass.

"Yeess," she said, barely awake.

"I need to talk to you about something."

Claire was pulled close and held tightly. Popping her eyes open, she knew something was wrong. She heard it in Nic's voice earlier on the phone. Twisting around, she faced Nic and studied her face.

"What's wrong?"

"I need to tell you something." Nic didn't make eye contact with her. In fact, there wasn't any joy in the eyes she'd loved for the past three years. They were fathomless and unreadable. "I don't know how to say this so I'm...I mean I wished I told you earlier...I feel like such a..."

Claire's heart sunk. "You want to break up." There was no emotion in Claire's voice, just a realization that perhaps somewhere it was something she thought might happen once Nic graduated from NPS. Nic had relayed to her that some of the guys were talking about the "four D's" and now they would fall victim to it too. No one left NPS unscathed.

"What? No, how could you even think that?" Nic sat up, crossed her legs, and avoided looking at her. Something was definitely wrong.

"What's wrong and don't tell me nothing. It's in your voice, and you won't even look at me." Claire tried to cover Nic's nakedness with the sheet, but it was either her or Nic, so she covered Nic. Always the mother.

"Come here." Nic opened her arms wide, waiting.

Sitting in Nic's lap, Claire laid her head against her chest, listening to the beating heart tapping out a quick rhythm that sped up the minute she touched Nic.

"The commandant called me into his office today."

"To apologize for being such an asshole?"

"Not exactly." Nic cleared her throat and stiffened. "I've come down on orders to Afghanistan." Nic blurted out.

Claire sat stunned at the news.

Afghanistan.

She couldn't wrap her mind around what Nic had just said. They'd been so far removed from that part of the military, enjoyed being settled, and started to build their new lives in Monterey. Claire was supposed to start school in the fall, Grace was going to first grade, they had looked at houses, and their lives were finally becoming normal. They could finally get married and plan a future, only now that future was Afghanistan.

"Claire?"

"Huh?" Claire's world collapsed in on her, she struggled to breathe, and suddenly the crickets...she could hear crickets. Funny, she'd never paid attention before, but now she heard them. "What'll I tell Grace? She's already lost one parent and now—"

"Claire, don't talk like that." Her body was squeezed tight, she felt tears threaten to fall, and finally they did, streaming down her face, falling on to her breasts. She shivered as the cold fog eked over the bay into the trees that surrounded their house. Looking at the billowing white wet, she thought it was more like a Hitchcock movie, ready to consume their bodies and leave nothing behind.

Focus, she thought. Her chest hurt...odd.

"Claire?"

Nic wiped at her tears, acting as if she could stop them just by willing them to be gone. She felt Nic dab at them with a corner of the sheet, but she couldn't get ahead of the flow. She dabbed continuously until Claire grabbed her hand, stopping her.

"Why?"

Nic knew what the question meant and Claire had every right to ask.

Nic bowed her head and teased the corner of the sheet, pulling at an errant thread.

"I can't go through this again, Nic. I can't."

"I know." She still didn't look up at Claire. "I don't have a choice in this, Claire. It's my payback to the Marine Corps."

"But I thought you were going to do research here?"

Nic shrugged and then sighed. "So did I."

"What happened?"

"I don't know. I have a call into the research department, but I wanted you to know as soon as possible."

"I don't know what to say, I mean—we had plans, I was going to go back to school. It was my turn, Nic."

"I know, I'm so sorry," Nic said, in barely a whisper, bowing her head.

Nic tried to grab her hands, but Claire yanked them back. She was too stunned to be coddled right now. She bordered on furious, and yet a part of her knew she needed to be supportive of Nic. She just wasn't in that space, not yet.

Chapter Six

Six weeks before the explosion.

"Don't cry, baby." Nic wiped again at the tears streaming down Claire's face. She felt her own resolve about to crumble. The last time she left for a combat zone, she was alone and actually looking forward to the adventure. Her flying days were far behind her and now she was faced with a different job in a war zone that wasn't as forgiving, if a combat zone could be called forgiving.

"I've got my computer, my phone, and my tablet. If I can't find a way to talk to you, I'll get on a landline over there and call collect. I promise." Nic had no idea what the technology bubble looked like in Afghanistan, but she been told that if you wanted to pay for it, technology abounded, even at the FOB's, forward operating bases, where the USO had tents with computers and phones.

Nic pulled Claire close and rested her lips on her forehead. "I love you so much. Every night you look at the stars in the sky, I'll be looking at the same stars and thinking about you and Grace. Every time a star falls from the sky, I'll be making a wish for a long, happy marriage." Nic picked up the small band and diamond she'd put on Claire's finger only hours before. They'd slipped off to city hall and made it permanent with a promise to have a big wedding when Nic got back.

She'd hang on to the promise, knowing she'd make it right when she returned.

"I love you so much," Claire said, kissing the top of Nic's head.

"I made you a promise and I plan on keeping it, so call Jordan and get busy on that wedding. I want to have the biggest celebration of marriage and see the most beautiful woman walking down that aisle to me."

"Me too."

Nic could barely swallow around the lump in her throat. She choked back tears, her quivering lip the only sign she was breaking down. She needed to be strong for Claire, for Grace, who'd fallen asleep in the back seat, for them.

"God...I'm gonna miss you so much, baby," Nic whispered as she clutched Claire tighter to her chest. At this moment in time she hated her job, she hated that she had to leave, but most of all she hated what this was doing to Claire one more time, in another world, in another war, but the same life.

"Come home to me, Colonel." Claire ran her hand softly down Nic's face, kissing her lips so tenderly that Nic felt her body melting into Claire's.

"I will. I promise."

"Don't make promises you can't keep."

Nic kissed the back of Claire's hand and then turned it over and kissed her palm. Rubbing her cheek against it, she whispered, "I'm coming home, Claire. I promise."

A knock on the window made Nic jump.

"Ready to go, Colonel?"

"Give me a minute."

"See you inside." The young Marine tossed a wave at Claire. "Ma'am."

Claire tossed her chin in his direction and then looked at Nic. A look that broke Nic's heart. She ached to take the pain away, but she couldn't. Time was the only thing that would bring them peace. The sooner time passed, the sooner she could get back home and start her new life.

"I've got to go, Mrs. Caldwell."

"Mrs. Caldwell? We haven't talked about that yet." Claire smiled.

"I know, but it's how I'll think of you every night, my wife, my life, my love." Nic grimaced and rubbed at her eyes, wiping away the tears that couldn't be stopped.

"Oh baby…I…love you…so much," Claire said, crying with Nic.

"Me too."

Nic kissed Claire for the last time and turned to get out, but Claire stopped her.

Nic laid her hand on Claire's and waited for a moment and then stepped out of the car, put her cover on, and scooped up her duffle and tech bag. She walked a few feet before she turned and blew Claire a kiss and stole one last look at her wife before she stepped inside the terminal.

Nic sat on the transport listening to nothing as noise bounced around the inside of the plane. This leg of the trip was different than the first leg of their flight in the civilian 737. That plane had flight attendants, drinks, and light casual conversation amongst a sea of multi-cam, desert digis, and soldiers who were still days away from Afghanistan. This leg, though, was vastly different, same soldiers but on the last leg of their flight to the combat zone. In Germany, they'd been given their weapons, ammo, and plates. Nic felt like she was a small forward for her favorite football team. The bulk of her battle gear reminded her that her mission was different this deployment. Small conversations barely able to be heard were shared between seatmates. Headphones dangled from most of those suddenly not interested in making small talk. A few had phones out showing pictures of kids or girlfriends that had been left behind. These photos and short videos would sustain them through their deployment.

Everyone had or wanted someone to go home to. Sadly, the young single guys had compartmentalized themselves together. They were young, lacked rank, and lived as if life back home didn't exist. These soldiers spent their time playing video games or sent out snapshots of each other on social media. Nic felt sorry for the young recruits. They had no idea what they were flying into. Their only thought was that they were protecting their family and the American way of life from foreign bodies that wanted to take it away from them. They all had the same values, the same fight, the same need to protect what was theirs. Nic wondered when she'd changed and something bigger than herself became more important. Her fight was gone a long time ago, probably in Iraq when she'd almost been killed in that helicopter crash. After that, she'd made different choices in her life and Claire and Grace were a result of that value system.

Nic grabbed the bench seat; her body bounced through the turbulence, making it harder for her to write in her journal, but she didn't care. Claire had given it to Nic as a going away gift.

"I want you to tell me what Afghanistan is like. Tell me what you're thinking, share that part of your life with me." Claire smiled and rubbed Nic's hand as she took the leather bound book.

"I'm not much of a writer."

"For me?"

Nic smiled and ran her fingertips along Claire's jaw, pulling her in for a kiss. The long, sensual taste of Claire made Nic tingle.

"For you, I'd part the sea even if the only reward was a kiss."

"You're such a romantic."

"Hmm, don't tell anyone."

"My lips are sealed as long as you keep kissing them."

"I think that can be arranged." Claire pulled Nic's collar and licked her upper lip, begging for more.

Now Nic wanted to leave something, her thoughts, snapshots of her time in Afghanistan, just in case something happened to her. She wanted Claire to know she'd thought of her and longed for her every day, every moment and that her last writings would be of Claire and Grace.

The wawawa vibration from the engines created a pattern that she learned to adjust to as she wrote. She'd never been one to keep a journal or a personal record of events in her life, but now she had a family and she had a need deep down to suddenly record what was going to happen. She wanted Claire and Grace to know what her life was like on deployment. Warts and all. Hopefully, it was nothing like Claire and Grace would ever experience, if Nic was lucky.

Nic looked up to see a kid staring at her. He

looked away when she locked eyes with him. She wondered what he saw when he looked at her; was she just another officer to salute, or did he see something different? She could only wonder. Going back to her journal, she put a few words down, looked at them, crossed two out and added a few more, looked at it again and then added another two lines. Her brow furrowed as she realized she'd written a poem. Nothing earth shattering, but it was Claire. Her vibrant light, her strength, her ability to love through loss, just a few lines that worked.

Nic wasn't the mushy, romantic type like Claire, but she told herself she owed it to Claire. Claire who would wait for her, Claire who had opened herself and her family to Nic. Claire who accepted Nic with all her baggage.

Saint Claire.

She owed Claire everything and all Claire had to do was ask and it was hers, so a journal dedicated to the love of her life was…doable.

Nic suddenly turned the page and stared at the blank white starkness of a new page. A metaphor in some way for her own life, a new page, a new phase, and now a new experience in Afghanistan. God, she was getting sappy. Maybe keeping a journal wasn't such a great idea. She slapped it closed and ran her fingers over the fresh leather. Pulling it to her nose, she inhaled its rich smell. It would lose its leather luster, and take on the worn life it had been purchased for, it would carry her secrets, and her desires, it would hold all she'd experienced in a place she didn't want to be, but most importantly – if something happened to her, Claire would know she had been the last thing on Nic's mind.

With another look around the plane, Nic noticed the same fresh-faced kid was staring at her again. Most of the soldiers scattered around him had found some peace in sleep. Moving around in their battle gear was hot, cumbersome, and a pain in the ass if truth be told. She'd had to pee for an hour, but the thought of trying to navigate the vest, gun on her hip, and other accoutrements of her attire left her less than ready to tackle the bathroom. She offered a brief, flat smile and then tucked her journal inside her backpack, zipped it, and pushed it under her seat. Now she'd wrestle the gear for the sake of her bladder.

Resettling back into her seat, she adjusted her gear one last time, settled her weapon in her lap and pulled out her journal and her headphones to drown out the noise. She wanted to jot down a few more thoughts down before she landed and all hell broke loose.

"Colonel, I understand you've seen combat before," said the fresh-faced Marine Corporal she noticed watching her before. Looking at him, she wondered what about her body language said, *I'm a chatter*, as he sat next to her. She noticed his nametag, *Swicatowski*. The damn thing was so long it went from edge to edge across his pocket, leaving no room for a border like most nametags.

Tucking her notebook inside her tech bag, she was annoyed at being disturbed. Pulling out an earplug, she looked over at the kid and sighed. "Is there is a question in there somewhere, Corporal?"

"No, Ma'am. Well, maybe, I was just wondering what it was like."

War was ugly business and yet some young guns thought this wasn't just their duty, this was their calling. Killing people who were threatening to take away their way of life, thousands of miles away. *Christ.* He was a little too excited for what lay before him. She took casual glance around the plane. Most of the soldiers were dressed in their battle gear. A collection of Marines, and Army, sat stoically, a few listened to music, most slept, and she ended up with the one kid who had insomnia.

"It's dirty, hot, and nothing I'd wish for my worst enemy."

Undeterred by the short answer, he plugged along. "Where were you stationed?"

Sizing him up, she didn't think he was the type for taking advice so she wasn't going to offer any. He didn't want it anyway. He wanted to march into the field with his M4 strapped to his chest, ready for action. He wanted to rid the world of the evil that he thought existed in a world where people still had dirt for carpet, mud for walls, and a person's worldly possessions could be carried in a cart. How do you explain that world to a snot-nosed kid who had more net worth than a tribe of people combined?

"Iraq."

"Oh wow, that was a long time ago," he said. She wanted to smack his cheery smile right off his freckled face. "I mean…" His head bobbed and he shrugged his shoulders. A pink rue colored his cheeks. "It was a few years ago, right?"

"Yep." She leaned back, crossed her arms over her the plate over her chest and closed her eyes, dismissing the kid.

"Well, I should let you get some sleep, ma'am."

He walked over to a seat next to someone who punched him in the arm and whispered, "What are you doing? Geez, that's an officer, know your place, dude."

"What? She puts her pants on just like us. Besides, I heard she was in combat before, I just wanted to know what it was like."

"Swicatowski, you don't think do you, man."

"Fuck you." He dipped his hat down, covering his eyes, and got comfortable in the hard seat.

Nic could only shake her head and hope she'd seen the last of the kid; he'd be a liability in whatever unit he was in if he didn't grow up quick.

"Buckle up, boys and girls, we are on final. Welcome to the sand box and thank you for flying United States Air. God bless you all and be safe over here." A voice blasted, barely drowning out the engines of the C130. The smiling, talking, or listening to music were replace with solemn faces, all with the sudden realization that they were back in a combat zone. Most of them had probably been in at least one, but a few fresh faces belied their inexperience, including the corporal who had tried to strike up a conversation.

All interior lights were extinguished and Nic felt the nose pitch forward, not the usual three percent glide path commercial pilots used on the first leg of her journey. This would be a combat entry - fast, quick, and dirty. She'd been briefed that lately the Taliban had taken to living with the local population around military bases so they could get closer access to landing aircraft. If they couldn't shoot them down, they'd been using high-powered lasers trying to blind the pilots and crash the planes. So the Air Force had to adjust to the circumstances and the bumpy landing and short stop suddenly made Nic thankful she didn't have to fly the big birds.

Before the back door dropped down and puked its cargo on the tarmac, Nic could feel the sweltering heat. Her long sleeve digital combat top she had worn in Iraq was replaced with a long sleeve digi nylon shirt that wicked the sweat off her body. This was a good thing; since putting in the plates of her body armor back in Germany, she was sweating like a pig. Nic looked around at the rest of the soldiers. It seemed that the Marines were the only ones still using the desert digital pattern. The Army had moved away from the digital pattern and it made them easier to spot. Then there were the international forces; hell, who had time to remember all the nations that were going to be at Camp Leatherneck?

Disembarking the C130, she heaved her duffle on her back, grabbed her technology bag, and slipped her hand around the grip of her issued M4. As she hit the asphalt, the heat slapped her in the face. It had to be at least 110 degrees out and it was past midnight. *God, what was it like during the day?* She wondered.

"Lt. Colonel Caldwell. Welcome," a short sergeant said, thrusting out his hand and grabbing Nic's tech bag. "Let me take some of this for you," he offered.

"Thanks. Is it always this hot at night?" Nic wiped at the perspiration dotting her upper lip.

"Oh, you think this is hot. Just wait," he said, almost too cheery.

"I'll take you to your CHU and you can get some shut-eye before meeting the Colonel." Tossing her duffle in the Humvee, he slid into the driver's seat and slammed the door. Nic stared at the oversized Humvee, wondering what the hell a CHU was.

"What's a CHU?" She said, adjusting her sidearm

and tucking the muzzle of her M4 between her legs.

"Oh, sorry. When was the last time you were in a combat zone?" he said, yanking on the wheel.

"About five years, Iraq."

"Oh, wow. Okay, well a CHU is a compartmentalized housing unit; it's just basically a glamorous name for a shipping container with a rack, air conditioning, a window, desk, and a locker. You're lucky, you get one all to yourself."

"Hmm." Nic looked out the window as they passed through another manned gate. A tall wall extended as far as Nic could see, with the typical razor wire winding around and across the top of it. A small city, crawling with people even at this late hour, buzzed with action.

"Good news is that it's lit up with internet so you can stay in contact with the home folks. Of course it's gonna cost ya, but hell, it's worth it on the late nights you when you get lonely and want to talk to the hubby. I'm sure you've been given the security briefing about all communication traffic being monitored, so those late night talks with your hubby might—"

"I don't have a husband." Nic stopped his rambling before he said something he might regret.

"Oh, boyfriend, gotcha."

"No boyfriend either."

The sergeant gave her a puzzled expression as he purposely looked down at the still sparkling ring on her left hand.

She returned his gaze and raised an eyebrow. If her stare down didn't convince him to mind his own business, her defiant look told him to drop the question.

"So, what's your job here, Colonel?"

He was a little too nosey for his own good and she wasn't in the mood to play twenty questions with someone she was sure was the base gossip. So, she gave the same answer she gave anyone who thought they should know her business.

"It's classified."

"Oh, gotcha." He yanked the wheel and skidded to a stop, kicking up dust. "Well, here we are, check in."

Headquarters had a few lights on still. The OD, Officer of the Day, was probably sitting at a desk, trying to catch a few winks before the day broke and all hell broke loose.

"Thank you, Sergeant."

"I'll wait for ya. It's my job to take you to your quarters."

"NCO on duty?"

"Yep."

"Okay, I'll process in and see you in a few."

"You got it. Take your time."

Grabbing her tech bag, she wiped her brow again, slipped her cover back on, and settled herself, ready for her assignment to be over. She flinched as small arms fire, somewhere over the wall, echoed throughout the base.

She was definitely back in combat, again.

Chapter Seven

Jordan whirled through the airport like a tornado kicked up tumble weeds in the desert. Men couldn't help themselves as she strutted past them; their eyes followed the swishing hips back and forth as she passed them.

"Poor bastards, if they only knew she didn't bat for their team. They'd be switching jerseys," Claire thought, smiling as Grace went wild seeing Auntie Jordie.

"Auntie, auntie." Grace ran towards Jordan, arms wide open.

"Hey, sweet stuff," Jordan said, tossing her carry-on to the floor. "I've missed you. Look at you, you've gotten so big, baby girl."

"I'm not a baby, Auntie Jordan."

"No, you sure aren't." Jordan winked at Claire and held Grace away from her, Grace's legs still firmly wrapped around her waist. "You're almost as grown up as I am."

Grace swung herself closer and wrapped her arms around Jordan's neck. "I'm not that old, Auntie Jordan."

"What? Are you calling me old?"

"Yep." Grace kissed Jordan on the lips. "You're as old as mommy."

"Speaking of mommy...How are you, kitten?"

Claire smiled and wondered when Jordan would

acknowledge her. They'd been friends since college and the only link to Claire's past that she allowed to hang around.

"I'm good. Thanks for coming," Claire said, weaving her arm through Jordan's to give her a half hug.

"You look tired. Not sleeping?" Jordan shifted Grace to her back, bent over, and picked up her carry-on. "Ready to go for a ride?" She peeked over her shoulder at Grace.

"Yeah, a piggy back ride."

"Where does she get all this energy?"

"I wish I knew," Claire said, grabbing the rolling bag and swatting Grace's behind. "Let's get your bag and get home."

"Bags."

"Bags, as in more than one?"

"Hey, you know me. I need it all."

"Uh huh, we do have stores here, you know?"

"Well, at least this is a better place than Pendleton," Jordan said as she galloped down the walkway with a squealing Grace.

"Oh yeah," Claire agreed. Monterey was definitely a step up, in her book, from Pendleton. "I'm glad you're here. I need a second opinion on a few houses I'm looking at."

"What?" Jordan slowed down and galloped back to Claire.

"I'm buying a house," Claire said, pulling Grace from Jordan as they watched baggage start to spit out on the revolving carousel.

"Does Nic know?"

"Does she need to?" Claire didn't look at Jordan. She'd made her decision when Nic had told her she was on orders to Afghanistan. She liked the area and she wanted to stay. Besides, it was her money from Mike's SGLI, Service members Government Life Insurance policy. She didn't need Nic's permission, it wasn't *her* money. Besides, she had become too wifely, lately. She'd acquiesced her own power, settling into a nice comfortable role as wife and mother and she needed to gain back her independence. Nic would just have to understand; besides, they had agreed during a night of pillow talk that a house was in their future and that if Claire wanted to start the process while Nic was away, Nic was fine with it. Claire was just doing the legwork for Nic. She knew the only reason Nic had encouraged it was to give Claire something to do while Nic was gone. Well, she was going to do just that, find them a house, and buy it.

"Well...doesn't Nic get a say in that decision?"

"She didn't ask me about going to Afghanistan," Claire huffed.

"She didn't have a choice, did she?" Jordan looked confused.

Claire shrugged. No, Nic didn't have a choice, but then neither did Claire. Pulling Jordan's luggage behind her, she was determined to make Nic's time overseas work for her, and the new semester at CSUMB started soon, so she didn't have time to waste. Determination was the word for the next six months.

Chapter Eight

"So, welcome to Camp Leatherneck, Colonel Caldwell."

Nic lowered her salute and accepted the hand extended. "Thank you, sir."

Nic studied the leathered face of the one-star standing in front of her. "Let me give you the ten cent tour around the base."

Beads of sweat were already rolling down between her shoulder blades and it was only o-seven-hundred. She didn't want to be disrespectful, but she'd seen all she needed to see last night, when it was still sweltering.

"Did the sergeant get you all settled in last night?"

"Yes, sir, thank you."

"How's your CHU?" he asked,

She smiled at him because he knew she wouldn't say anything about the metal shed that doubled for a sleeping unit. It was only a tad bit better than her accommodations when she was over in Iraq, but it was a *rack with a sack*, as she often called it in Iraq. Some place to rest her head while her body recovered from the torturous heat, and the vibration of her helicopter. This time she wouldn't be in a chopper, but she remembered the sweltering temperature like it was yesterday.

"I'm sure with a few pictures scattered around it

will feel just like home."

"Well, if you can make that happen, you're a better person than I am. I've been in this shit hole for a while now, Colonel, and you can't dress up a turd. Just sayin'."

"I appreciate your honesty, sir." Good, at least she didn't have to lie.

"Your civilian is here, good luck with that one. He's only been here a couple of days and he's already pissed off the cooks in the chow hall, a couple of the NCOs are ready to throw a blanket party in his honor, and I think he was expecting Hilton accommodations. Seems he doesn't like his CHU."

"Great," she said, adjusting her gear.

"I'm not really your chain of command, you answer to D.C., but I like to keep a tight ship. If you run into any problems with him, let me know. I know you're here to do some kinda research on the tribal leaders and shit, but if you have any questions I'm not here for that."

"I understand."

"He said something about hooking up with you at the chow hall. If you want to catch him now, though, I saw him going into the USO tent."

"No, I'll catch him at the chow hall. Maybe he'll be in a better mood after he talks to his wife."

"He's got internet in his CHU, so he isn't there for that."

"Hmm." Nic just grunted her response. She already didn't like her civilian counterpart if he'd succeeded in pissing off the General.

Walking around the motor pool, Nic couldn't help but notice the different Humvees, some with huge arms extending out in front of them, some bulked up with armor, gun mounts on the top of most, and some had some sort of netting around them.

"These are definitely different than my tour over in Iraq." Nic pointed at the array of vehicles.

"Yep, we've gotten smarter about our transports. I'll give you a quick rundown, 'cause you might have to be living in one of these for the next six months." General James walked around some soldiers waist deep in a Humvee. Pointing at one with elaborate framework sticking out past the front of the Humvee, wheels attached to the front, he said, "This one is called a mine roller. It's designed to explode an IED before the Humvee hits it." He walked over to another modified Humvee and patted the hood, its armament sticking about ten feet in front of the Humvee. "You probably saw something like this in Iraq. The metal plate triggers the IED heat seeking sons-of-bitches. These bastards have gotten good at killing us and we're barely one step ahead of 'em most of the time." Pointing to a grouping of Humvees, he said, "A couple of these probably have thicker armor than the ones you used in Iraq." He pointed at a few others and explained their uses. "The problem is still the same, though; the damn things are easier than hell to flip, so if the explosions don't kill us, the damn rollover just might."

"What about those?" Nic said, pointing to one with netting all over it.

"Aw, those have an RPG netting wrapped around the Humvee. It's got tiny explosive gaps pinned through the screen and the missiles explode before hitting the vehicle."

"Wow, no shit?"

"No shit." General James walked over to the

Humvee and fingered the netting. "Casualties are down, thanks to all of this new technology. Those little bastards are using remote controlled cars to carry their IED, or a cell phone can detonate an IED right when we get over it, so we're just trying to stay one step ahead, but sometimes I wonder."

"Some things never change, sir."

His smile barely broke the cracked, sunburnt skin of his face. War was hard on people and it showed on their faces. The stress of constantly trying to stay alive in a combat zone, lost sleep, and the dust and heat of the desert wore a person down. Like sandpaper, its abrasive nature couldn't be reversed, hence all of the PTSD cases lingering in the VA hospitals. Nic only hoped that six months would fly by and it wouldn't show on anything but her DD 214 when she left the military.

"I've assigned Sgt. Ramirez to you for your excursions into the tribal areas. She's a 240 Bravo gunner."

"A female?" Nic questioned. Where they were going wasn't any place for…Nic stopped herself before she finished the thought. What the fuck was she thinking? Only men were capable of shouldering a machine gun, only men could protect her and her civilian? She shook her head; if she could kick her own ass, she'd bend over. This wasn't a place for any of them, period.

"Colonel, are you telling me you'd rather be cooped up with two men in a Humvee like that?" he said, pointing to one of the few missing any forward apparatus. "If so, I can change the orders and assign a male to you."

"No, a female is perfect. My apologies, sir, I

didn't mean anything by it. I just assumed there weren't any females assigned to the base."

"We only have about fifteen in the Cavalry unit here. But you'll find them throughout the base and at the FOBs." He stroked the stubble on his chin so hard it sounded like sandpaper against his rough hand. "I'll send her over to your CHU and you can get acquainted. Probably a good idea that she meets you before that civilian pain in the ass."

"Didn't score any points, did he?"

"I don't have time for candy asses and I can spot one a mile away. Good luck with him, Colonel. He isn't going to travel well and I suspect that your bitch meter is going to peak out quick with that one."

"Thanks for the heads up."

God, could this deployment get any worse, Nic thought, running her sleeve across her forehead.

Chapter Nine

"This little number is hands down the best deal on the market for the money," the realtor said as she swung the front door wide and made a theatrical sweep of her arm. "After you, now don't forget you're only about three-quarters of a mile from the beach."

"What the fuck, is this the closet for the house next door?" Jordan whispered in Claire's ear. "My walk-in at home is bigger than this cracker jack box."

"Shh, let's look around before we cast aspersions." Claire followed the high heels clicking on the wooden floors.

"The backyard is fantastic. This just came on the market. The children of the woman who owned it live in Minnesota and they don't really get to California. I tried to tell them that renting it would give them positive cash flow, but oh well, their loss is your gain. Right?"

They moved from room to room until they were through the house in less than two minutes. A quick walk through was understandable, considering it was all of about nine hundred square feet. The carpet was an ugly green shag, a holdover from the seventies, the wallpaper was...well, it was ugly, Claire thought as she stepped down the rickety wooden stair to the back yard.

Her cell phone vibrated, signaling she'd received

an email from Nic. How did she know? Nic was the only alert she'd set on her phone, for good reason. She didn't want to miss anything from her wife halfway around the world. Tapping the screen, she read the message.
Wanna Skype tonight 6:00 pm your time.
God, I miss you.
Love N

She'd rush home right now and sit in front of the computer for the next few hours if it meant she could see her wife, even if only for a few minutes. Smiling, she tucked her phone and looked around the microscopic backyard.

"What the hell is this?" Jordan said way too loudly.

"Well, this is the backyard," the realtor said, twirling around on the thick green carpeted grass. "These are mature fruit trees that are so heavy with fruit every year...well, they just cover the ground. Do you make jam? Or perhaps you can fruits and vegetables. Well, as you can see, there's plenty of room for a garden."

"Are you kidding me, where?" Jordan said, sidestepping overgrown trees and shrubs that hadn't seen pruning in years, maybe a decade. "You said this woman's kids don't get to California. They let their mother live like this? They should be ashamed of themselves." Jordan brushed something off her shoulder and then squealed. "Spider, spider, shit."

"Hold still," Claire said, just as Grace started screaming. "What are you screaming for?"

"Auntie Jordan has a spider on her. Get it, mommy. Get it."

"Yeah, mommy." Jordan pulled at her hair and

then shivered. "Did you get it?"

Claire sighed. "There wasn't anything on you, honey."

"I felt it. You saw it, didn't you, pumpkin," Jordan said, picking up Grace. "Let's get out of here. We'll meet you in the car."

"Thanks." Claire suddenly regretted bringing Jordan along. "So, what's the asking price?"

"It's a steal," the real estate broker said, putting her hands on Claire's shoulders, guiding her back inside.

"What's a steal going for these days?"

"Well, it's only six hundred and fifty thousand dollars. It's in the best school district and don't forget you're only three-quarters of a mile from the beach."

"Yes, I remember."

While she could swing it with the life insurance from Mike's death, she wasn't so sure the cold, foggy coast was where she wanted to live. Looking up, she noticed that very blanket rolling over her and it was only one in the afternoon.

"Do you have anything in the Salinas area, maybe Corral de Terra, somewhere warmer?"

"Honey, there's lots of property out there, but are you sure you and your daughter wouldn't be comfortable here? Pacific Grove is such a desirable location and you know what they say—location, location, location."

"Yes, well, it isn't just my daughter and myself, my wife will be joining me when her tour in Afghanistan is over."

Silence passed between them, but only for a few heartbeats.

"Oh, I love the gays. In fact, some of my best

friends are gay men. They are just fabulous. Do you know Dr. Hendricks and his husband Carl?"

"No, I'm afraid I don't." The typical, *oh you're gay, so you must know so-and-so because they're gay.*

"Hmm, they're very active in the community. They host this wonderful event for charity at their home. It's just lovely. I sold them the property and then Carl just..." She threw her hands around. "Well, he just turned that into a gem. Not that it wasn't already, but you know how gay men can be, I mean they just have a way with interior design."

"Yes, they do, don't they." Claire suddenly wished she hadn't relied on a picture to pick her realtor. Looks could be so deceiving.

Moving closer to Claire, she put her hand on her arm and whispered, "I just want you to know I voted against Prop. 8. Travesty I tell you, a complete injustice."

"Hmm." Was all Claire could muster at the moment.

"Well, I can pull up some listings on my computer. I'll just look through our little website that has all the homes listed on it and we can jet over to the 68 corridor. There are just some wonderful homes over there."

Claire could swear she almost heard the sound of a cash register ringing as the woman looked down at her phone. A whistle caught her attention as Jordan motioned Claire over.

"Could you excuse me for a moment, please?"

"Of course, it will take me just a moment to bring up some listings. Go head, I'm right behind you," she said, shooing Claire.

"What?"

"Grace has an upset stomach," Jordan said without looking at her.

A lie. Jordan never looked at Claire when she lied.

"Are you sick, honey?"

Grace, sitting in her car seat strapped in and ready to go, grabbed her stomach and nodded.

"A bad tummy ache?"

Another nod and this time it was topped off with a groan for added affect.

"Okay, I'll let the realtor know."

Just as she walked away, she turned and saw Jordan and Grace high-fiving. *Stinkers!*

Chapter Ten

The sounds of a small city getting active permeated the metal walls of Nic's CHU. She'd spent a few minutes jotting down a few paragraphs in her leather bound notebook. She was determined to keep her mind active and not sit around letting her thoughts eat at her. She was restless, ready to get started and get this tour over. She wondered what Claire and Grace were doing at this very moment. Sunday was their day. A day reserved for lying in bed, reading to Grace, eating bagels Nic had picked up the night before, and just relaxing. Around noon, they'd pack everything up and make their way to the walking path around the beach. One time they'd walked all the way down to the lighthouse in Pacific Grove. How they'd gotten that far was a testament to Grace's sleeping ability in a stroller and their ability to talk about everything and anything. Nic loved days like that, time with her family, doing what families around the world did, be together. God, she was heart sick; home sick would have been easy, but she missed her lover and her heart ached for Claire.

A pounding on the door jerked Nic around. What the fuck? Nic stood and with three steps was pulling the door to her CHU wide.

"Yeah," she said tersely.

"Sorry, I'm looking for Colonel Caldwell."

"You found her. Where's the emergency,

Sergeant?"

"Colonel, my apologies. I'm just used to...Sgt. Ramirez, ma'am." Sgt. Ramirez saluted smartly.

"Relax, Ramirez. Come on in."

"Ma'am?" Her discomfort was visible.

"Well, it's either in here where it's cooler or out there and we both sweat like pigs. Up to you."

"Out here, ma'am."

"Fine."

Nic understood the implications of two women, one an officer and the other enlisted, being in an enclosed room. She couldn't deny that tongues would wag, no matter the consequences. She'd found herself in similar situations and always opted to leave the door open, unless she was counseling one of her Marines on a personal issue.

Ramirez stood at parade rest, but still ramrod straight. She wasn't wearing her battle gear, instead the nylon camo shirt the Army had adopted, with a sidearm strapped to her thigh. The Army called it their Army Battle shirt. From the looks of it, the Army had ditched the digital camo patterns for a more functional multi-camo pattern. There was still no consistency between the services, which made life a little easier for Nic to figure out who all the players were and who belonged to whom.

Nic quickly assessed Ramirez; her medium stocky-build looked like she could take on any man. Broad shoulders, thick neck, and good-sized arms were all a testament to the job she did in the Army. Carrying around a twenty-five pound machine gun and ammo, on top of her battle gear, didn't make for girlie girls. Her uniform was clean, and serviceable. Her boots wore the requisite amount of dust and still looked almost new. Her cap was exactly the right distance above the eyebrows and her brown hair was tucked neatly under it. No makeup meant she either didn't have time for it, or she just wasn't the type, and chapped lips denoted the harsh environment and that Ramirez probably wasn't drinking enough water.

"So Sergeant. Shall we at least go to the chow hall and get some coffee? Check that, how about something cold to drink." Nic swung her hand in the direction of the chow hall.

"Yes, ma'am." Ramirez waited for Nic to start walking before she followed.

"So Sergeant. Where you from?"

"California, ma'am."

Short clipped answers. Nic was used to those, but if they were going to be bunking together in a Humvee, Ramirez would need to get over the whole rank thing.

"What's your first name, Sergeant?"

"C.C., ma'am."

"C.C. short for something?"

"Yes, Ma'am."

Nic sighed; pulling teeth on a bull would be an easier exercise.

"What's it short for, Sergeant?"

"Cecilia, ma'am."

"Where in California, Sergeant?"

"South-central, ma'am."

South-central Los Angeles was a rough part of L.A., mostly gangs and drugs, with a smattering of good family who were stuck there through no fault of their own. Nic looked at Ramirez and wondered what her story was; everyone had a story in the military, even Nic.

"Monterey," Nic said, pointing to her chest.

"Nice."

Nic knew the reputation Monterey had as a playground for those that could afford it. Truth be told, if it wasn't for the Naval Postgraduate School, she doubted she could afford a life by the beach anywhere in California. She wasn't going to complain though; Monterey was definitely on her PCS list when she got out.

The chow hall almost seemed dim and chilly compared to the blinding sunlight and heat that was the desert. Pulling her sunglasses off, Nic searched the crowded room for something cold.

"This is the only chow hall open twenty-four hours. If you want something hot to eat, you have to wait for mealtime. Otherwise there are some sandwiches, candy bars, and other pre-made shit."

Nic couldn't help but notice the popularity of the ice cream machine and she suddenly had a craving for ice cream.

"Ice cream seems popular." Nic nodded at the line.

"Yeah, you should have seen the meltdown when the machine broke." Ramirez smiled at the joke and then it disappeared.

"Meltdown, cute."

Ramirez shrugged and walked over to a counter and pulled a water bottle from a bag slung across her chest. Filling it, she grabbed something else and walked to the cashier. The line should have been daunting to Nic, but ice cream was really sounding beyond satisfying. It was a comfort food of sorts for her, so she'd risk it. A man standing in front of her turned and barely acknowledged her as he checked her out. His eyes resting on silver oak leaf she wore, he suddenly stiffened and stepped to the side, motioning for her to go in front of him.

"I'm good, I can wait my turn. Thanks anyways," she said.

"Ma'am." Was the only acknowledgement he gave as he moved up in line.

Ten minutes, it had taken that long for Nic to get to the front and now she was surprisingly faced with a well-stocked ice cream bar. Every topping one could think of was filled to the brim and Nic noticed someone was constantly checking and restocking. Perhaps the meltdown when the machine went down had something to do with the constant attention. Nic knew how important morale was in a combat situation and something as simple as an ice cream machine taking such a role of importance wasn't surprising. Having lived on MREs, meals-ready-to-eat, for months was enough to make someone go postal. Her first hot meal had been nothing more than a burger and fries, but it was the best burger and fries she'd had in her life.

Topping off her bowl of ice cream with hot fudge, whip cream, and sprinkles, she resisted the red cherry. Those were always saved for Claire and Grace; to have one now would seem sacrilegious. She'd save it for when she got home.

Sliding into a chair across from Ramirez, she pushed her spoon across the top of the pile of ice cream and sighed; it was almost melancholy. Hesitating, she studied a drop of fudge ready to drop back down and join its buddies back in the bowl. Flicking her tongue out she caught it and shoved the spoon in her mouth. The sudden cold hit the top of her mouth and a brain freeze set in immediately. Closing her eyes, she savored the cold, chocolate luxury she was sure wouldn't be available to them soon enough.

"Guess you like ice cream," Ramirez said, jutting her chin at the overladen bowl.

"I might have gone a little overboard. Guess I was thinking I was still at home. My daughter and I usually share and for a six-year-old she's got a healthy appetite."

"So you got kids," Ramirez said, studying her intently. It was more of a statement than a question.

"One." Nic wasn't going to out herself to someone she didn't know. They both might bleed green but Nic had her share of homophobes in the military; she didn't want to know she was sleeping next to one out in the middle of nowhere.

"Well, we're pretty lucky here. You can Skype or send emails pretty regularly. Except when there is a KIA, then we go on lockdown. No communications out until the family is notified."

"Does that happen a lot?"

"What, lockdown?"

"KIA."

"Enough that you don't take your next breath for granted." Ramirez took a long pull off her water bottle.

"That's pretty stoic for someone so young." Nic licked the back of her spoon and savored the last few spoonfuls of melted ice cream.

"You grow up fast here, Colonel. If you don't, you make stupid mistakes that get others killed."

"Did that happen to you?"

Ramirez was still searching Nic's face when she looked away and answered.

"Not me."

"Someone you knew then." Nic had seen that look before; the loss was evident in her eyes. It was the one thing Nic couldn't put her finger on when she came to her door earlier. She wasn't that fresh faced corporal Nic had met on the flight over; in fact, she doubted Ramirez was ever a fresh faced enlistee. Something about her said life had lived her, not the other way around. Ramirez didn't answer, so she decided that she'd take a different line of questions.

"So Sergeant. I understand you're going to be accompanying me on these little jaunts out beyond the wall."

"Yes, ma'am."

"How long have you been stationed here?"

"Three months."

"First time here?"

"No, ma'am. It's my third deployment to a combat zone." Almost robotic, Ramirez sat straight up, her hands folded on the table.

"Three times to Afghanistan, who did you piss off?"

"I was over in Iraq the first time. I requested deployment all three times."

"I see, so you're a risk taker."

"I'm not sure I know what you mean, ma'am."

"Do me a favor, can we dispense with the ma'am stuff?"

Ramirez stared at Nic. She wasn't an open book; in fact, she was shut down tighter than a sea hatch on a submarine. "That's an order, Sergeant."

Still no expression. Nic knew she didn't couldn't make her comply, but she wanted to put Ramirez at ease. Frustrated, Nic wondered if she should keep trying to converse with Ramirez or let her keep her walls firmly intact.

"I won't keep you, Sergeant. I'll let you know when I make contact with the civilian we'll be working with and we can get together and map out where and when we'll be off base."

"Yes, ma'am." Ramirez stood up to leave and then turned towards Nic. "I'm glad to be working with you, ma'am," she said over her shoulder.

Nic only nodded at Ramirez. If that was happy, Nic would hate to see pissed.

※※※※

Nic checked her watch, booted up her computer, and checked her watch again. She was nervous. Why? She was just calling her lover. It wasn't like they had a fight, or she left on bad terms with Claire. If she was being honest with herself, she felt like a schoolgirl getting ready to go on her first date, again. Oh, what a disaster that had been. High school had been a confusing time for Nic, sorta. It was probably more confusing for the girls she'd had a crush on than herself, but confusion had a way of breeding and replicating itself in every adolescent schoolgirl. She was digressing. She wiped the screen of the thin layer of dust that had already accumulated there, not wanting anything to keep her from seeing her wife. Her wife, Claire was now her wife. She was still stunned by the fact that they had run off and gotten married by the justice of the peace. Yep, Claire was her wife and when she got back, she'd adopt Grace and make it all tidy and neat, the perfect family. Tapping her fingers on the desk, Nic couldn't wait to talk to Claire. Being in transit had postponed any face time they could have had, so Nic was relishing their first contact. It had only been a week, but it seemed more like a lifetime when you'd rather be somewhere else. She'd emailed her wife every day, but it couldn't replace that moment when she saw her face.

Some on deployment ticked off the days on a giant calendar; it was too painful for Nic to have a visual reference to her obligation. She'd had to wait a few days before her connection was live, but now she would talk to Claire anytime she was in her rack. The possibilities were endless, she thought as she tapped her mouse across the screen. Hitting the icon, she waited as the software did its thing, the red dots vibrating on the blue background. Her window expanded, her small face in the corner and Claire's filling her screen. Her body suffused with excitement looking at her lover in the flesh, sort of.

"Hi baby," she said, choking back the lump that had threatened to render her speechless. Yep, first date jitters all over again.

"Hey, sexy." Claire's voice melted her.

"Oh God, you look great."

"You're a sight for sore eyes." Claire smiled. "I was worried we won't get to talk and I'd have to be happy with a few emails."

"Me too, but they have so much technology over here, it's nothing like when I was in Iraq," Nic reassured Claire.

"God, I miss you already."

"Me too."

Nic cradled her face in her hands and stared at the screen. Claire was so close and yet she was so far away. She let her finger trail down the screen along

Claire's face.

"What're you doing, silly?"

"Touching you."

Nic could feel the tears building; she only hoped she could keep them from falling. This was harder than she thought it would be. God, she loved Claire. The next six months were going to be hell.

"Is that your place?" Claire picked up the slack in their conversation.

"Yeah, it's not much more than one of the shipping containers you see on the docks with some paneling and an air-conditioning unit over there." She tossed her head to the right.

"Show me."

"You wanna see this shit hole?"

"I what to make sure you're all right and if I see where you're living, I can think about you there and know that you're safe and I don't have anything to worry about. How about that?" Claire beamed.

"Okay, be prepared to be amazed. Don't say I didn't warn you."

"Duly noted."

Nic picked up her laptop and pointed it towards the back of her CHU. Then she turned it towards her bed and pointed it to the stuffed bunny resting on her pillow Grace had stuffed in her bag without her knowing. She opened her wall locker and dead center were pictures of them together. They were the first thing she'd put out.

"Oh my God, are those photos of us?"

Nic choked up. "Yeah."

Nic finished the short tour by putting the computer back on her desk and wiped her eyes.

"Oh baby. Are you okay?"

"Yeah..." she said. She cleared her throat and sniffed. "I'm good now that I get to talk to you."

"Come here." Claire motioned to the screen.

Puzzled, Nic moved closer. Lips covered the screen as Claire let out a smack. "There's a kiss for my beautiful wife."

"God, I miss you." Nic swiped at her eyes, blinking back tears. "This is harder than I thought."

"Do you want me to let you go?"

"Oh no, I want you stay right where you are. In fact, you don't have to say anything. Just let me sit here and look at you."

"Now you're being silly."

"Hmm, maybe. So tell me what you've been up to, did you get registered for classes?"

"I did. Well, I've been accepted. I need to wait for the spring semester to start before I can get started, but it looks good. How about you, what have you been up to?"

Nic raised her hand. "Oh 'bout five-eleven."

"Really, you've grown since the last time I've seen you."

They both laughed at the joke.

"So, what are you wearing?" Nic whispered.

"Jeans and a T-shirt, what, are you blind?" a voice off camera said.

"Hi Jordan." Nic blushed. Why? It wasn't as if what she said wasn't said to wives all over the deployment. Well, maybe not in some of the enlisted CHUs where they were bunked up three to a room, or the USO tent.

"Hi Nickie," Grace said, running into the frame. "I miss you, Nickie, when are you coming home?"

"Soon, pumpkin. Are you taking care of

Mommy?"

"Yep. We went shopping for a ho—" Claire clamped her hand over Grace's mouth and said something in her ear. "Oh, we went surprise shopping today."

"Oh, you did. Can you tell me what the surprise is?" Nic laughed, knowing Grace had probably been given a reprimand for saying anything about a surprise.

"Nope, mommy said I won't get a surprise if I tell you what a surprise is." Grace smiled and touched the screen. "You look like you're right here, Nickie."

"You look like you're right here, too. I thought when you said surprise you meant the surprise in my bag."

"Did you like your surprise?"

"I did. I'll sleep with Ms. Bunny every night."

"Can I say hi to Ms. Bunny?"

"Sure, hold on."

Nic grabbed the bunny and rushed back. "Hi, Grace. How are you?" Nic said, waving one of the bunny's paw.

"Ms. Bunny, you have to take care of Nickie, okay?"

"You bet." Nic pushed the bunny against the camera and blew Grace a kiss.

Grace smacked her hand against her lips and swung it away, blowing a kiss to Nic.

"I love you, pumpkin." Nic started to tear up again.

"I love you, Nickie, bye, talk to you later." With that, Grace was off and running. Nic could hear her tearing through the house, slamming a door behind her.

"So, what's the surprise?" Nic prodded Claire.

"It wouldn't be a surprise if I told you, would it?"

Nic squeezed her fingers together and said, "Hint?"

"Nope."

"Okay, I guess I'll have to wait."

"I guess you will." Claire's wicked smile left her wondering what was up.

Before she could say anything else, a pounding on her door made her jump.

"What the hell?"

"What's going on, baby?" Fear laced Claire's question.

"I don't know, someone's at the door and this better be good. Hold on a sec," she said, pissed someone was cutting in on her down time.

"Okay."

Nic pushed the door open and found herself peering down at the top of a bald head.

"Can I help you?"

"Colonel Caldwell?"

"Yes."

"Max Drummond, I'm the guy from D.C."

"Excuse me?"

"I'm the guy you're working with here in Afghanistan. I think you're working for me doing a tribal census."

"I think you have an incorrect impression of the chain of command, Mr. Drummond. I report to the United States Marine Corps, not a civilian."

"Hmm, I'm sorry, that came out all wrong. I mean we're working together to gather data on the interactions of the tribal groups and how we, I mean the United States, can help them get through this war."

"Mr. Drummond, can you and I meet in the USO tent and we can have this conversation and iron out the details then?" Nic was perturbed that he'd interrupted her first call with Claire and by the looks of it, he wasn't exactly instilling any confidence in the mission. At least not the mission she was briefed on.

"Of course, shall we say ten minutes?"

"I'll see you in half-an-hour. Make sure to bring all your materials for the mission."

"This isn't really a mission." He looked at Nic and then doubled back. "I mean it's more of data gathering so that D.C. can develop a plan of helping the tribal elders divest themselves of their relationships with the Taliban."

Steamed that she was wasting time with Mr. Drummond, she was short. "Half-an-hour, Mr. Drummond, and I'll bring the gunner who will be working with us."

"Wait, what? No, we don't need a gunner."

"Half-an-hour, Mr. Drummond."

"Colonel." Was all she heard as she slammed the door.

Nic settle herself on the chair and tried to relax. She wanted to talk to her wife and not some pencil neck from D.C.

"Honey, is everything all right?" Claire looked like she was trying to peek around the monitor to catch a glimpse of Nic. If she looked any cuter, Nic would be tempted to catch the next transport home and risk her career. Well, if it were only that easy.

"Hey baby. It was just the civilian I'm working with over here. He decided to pick right now to get together and go over the mission."

"Well, I should let you go then, so you can get

started on your job."

"I don't want to let you go, honey." Anxiety grabbed Nic; her chest was suddenly in a vise.

"It'll be okay, Nic. Why don't you send me a schedule of some times we can get online and I'll try and be alone next time." Claire smiled at the innuendo.

"Hmm, sounds like a plan. I'll email you when I'm done with this yahoo and see what we can set up. If you're on later, maybe we can connect again?"

"It's late here, but I'll try and stay up."

"No, no, it's all right. I forgot about the time difference. I'll email you. I should have a better idea of what my time looks like after speaking to this guy."

"I love you. Just remember that while you're out there. We'll be fine, so don't worry about us. Besides, Jordan is here and she'll keep me out of trouble." Claire tried to sound reassuring.

"Oh, that instills a hell of a lot of confidence." Nic laughed.

"I heard that, Nic. Just for that I'm gonna make sure she gets drunk and stupid this weekend."

Claire looked at the screen, shook her head, and mouthed, *No, she's not.*

"I love you."

"I love you, too. Now go and find that guy. Play nice with the man from D.C., Honey."

"Oh, I will. Hug Grace for me and tell Jordan I'm watching her."

"Oh, Nic," Jordan shouted somewhere behind Claire. "She'll behave. Besides, she's no fun without you."

"Bye Jordan." Nic blew Claire a kiss. "I love you."

"I love you, too."

The screen went blank almost as soon as Claire

said it. Timing is everything, Nic thought about the civilian, as she closed her laptop and grab her cover. Pulling out her pad, she wrote some notes down, closed it, and packed it back in her pocket, smoothing the closure down. Time to see the man from D.C.. Now she knew what the General meant when he said he called Mr. Drummond a candy ass. Could this get any worse?

Chapter Eleven

"Nic sounds good," Jordan said, still fingering her tablet.

"You think so? She sounded depressed to me."

Claire was worried about Nic. She looked like she hadn't slept in a week and from what she heard, Nic's temper was flaring. Something about this deployment wasn't sitting right with Claire. Nic had been promised a job at NPS and now she was overseas, basically doing data entry. That just wasn't right, but neither of them could do anything about it. Maybe she was just over reacting to the situation. It had been almost four years since Mike's death and the last time she'd had to deal with a spouse overseas she'd lost him. Did spouses suffer from PTSD? Was it possible that she was reacting to something from the past? She didn't know, but she needed a diversion or she'd worry herself sick.

"Well, she is overseas." Jordan poked at something on her tablet. "Hey, check out this house. It's on an acre, trees and plenty of room for kids, and it's a hell of a lot less than that hamster house we saw today."

"Hmm, let's see."

Claire sat next to Jordan, handing her a bottle of water. Tucking her feet under her, she settled in for what promised to be a longer night. Once Jordan got something stuck in her craw, she wouldn't let it go until she could cough it up. The realtor today had rubbed Jordan all wrong and she lectured Claire all the way home about vultures and used car salesmen. What they had to do with buying a house Claire was still trying to figure out, but Jordan would connect the dots for her in that weird little way she always did.

"Why don't you just move here and we can spend all our time doing girlie things—manie-pedies, shopping, brunch. We can buy a house next to each other and sit around and watch Grace grow up." Claire snuggled on Jordan's shoulder and teased her finger across the screen. "This looks nice."

"Hmm, and what about Nic? Does she do manie-pedies? I can just see Nic now with her toes in the little piggy separators, some guy massaging her calves and feet and then bright red polish. Gives me goose bumps." Jordan chuckled, swiping her finger across the screen. "Oh, this looks nice. How far are you willing to drive to get to school?"

"Nic can do manie-pedies. You should see her with Grace. Grace puts makeup on Nic and they do each other's nails. She puts cotton balls between Grace's toes and then paints them and then they have a little tea party afterwards."

"I saw that little invitation to a cocktail party on your frig, are you gonna go?"

"Meh, probably not." Claire pulled the tablet out of Jordan's hands and enlarged one of the houses on the screen.

"Why not?"

"Nic's not here and I don't like to go to those things alone. Besides, they're just a bunch of stuffed shirts and their wives. Well, there are a few really wonderful women, but for the most part they're living vicariously through their husband's careers and rank."

"I'll go with you. I love a party."

"Are you kidding?"

"No, besides, if Nic comes back and teaches here you don't want to burn any bridges with these people, do you?"

As much as a wife could hurt her husband's career being a bitch, she could also be an asset by being able to mix and mingle with the big wigs on the base. God, she hated it when Jordan was right. Nic was only going to be gone six months and the chances all of those at the party would still be here and influencing decisions made it tougher for Claire not to attend. Office politics sucked but military politics had to be worse. The military was insulated, a world unto its own, and regardless of what happened on the outside, the internal politics reverberated all the way to Washington D.C..

"Fine, when is it again?"

Jordan clapped her hands. "Oh yeah, this will be fun. We can play dress-up and get manie-pedies and everything."

"Lovely. I hope Nic appreciates this," Claire said, flicking through another set of images. This promised to be a disaster, she just knew it.

Chapter Twelve

Nic studied Ramirez, wondering more about her as she twirled a saltshaker. She'd caught Ramirez sitting on her rack staring at the top bunk while everyone around her chatted, shared photos, and talked about home life. Nic stood at the door and watched her until someone noticed her standing at the door. Everyone stood the minute she was noticed and Nic acknowledged their greeting, waiting to say anything to Ramirez until they were outside.

Ramirez shot out of bed, still wearing her combat shirt, pants, and boots. Did she ever relax? Now they sat in silence waiting for their civilian, Max Drummond.

"So, why a gunner?"

"Ma'am?"

"Why did you decide to be a gunner?" Nic was curious with all the M.O.S. in the Army why she picked being a 240 Bravo gunner.

"I like guns," she said without looking at Nic.

Sighing, Nic gave up. She'd tried to strike up a conversation, but Ramirez was clearly a private person. The best she could hope for was eventually Ramirez would loosen up enough to carry a conversation. If not, she would be stuck talking to Drummond for the next six months, and from the looks of the man, she'd rather have a root canal.

"Colonel, there you are, I got lost. I can't believe

how big this base is. All the buildings look the same and everyone is dressed alike so I couldn't get my bearings."

"Mr. Drummond, I'd like to introduce Sgt. Ramirez, she'll be the gunner on this mission."

"Gunner, oh no, we don't need a gunner."

Ramirez stood up and nonchalantly said, "Fine by me. I didn't want to have to save your asses anyway."

The response surprised Nic, but couldn't say anything before Ramirez started to walk away.

"Sergeant, stand down." Ramirez stopped dead in her tracks and didn't move. "Get over here and sit down." Nic pointed to the chair next to her, separating her from Max. Nic looked around and realized she might have said it too loud when all activity in the USO tent stopped. *Shit.* "Sit down, Mr. Drummond. Let's talk about how this is going to go." Nic commanded and at that, everyone at her table sat. Ramirez, visibly pissed, Drummond, his mouth still wide open.

Drummond set his briefcase on the table and opened it, taking out maps, papers, a pen, and a highlighter. He didn't look at anyone; he just opened the map and took out what appeared to be a calendar.

"I've laid out our work for the next few months. I've left a month open in case we need to go back out and re-interview any of the tribal elders. As we go through our notes we can assess what is viable and credible information and decide if we need to go back to a particular elder."

This was news to Nic. In her direct instructions from D.C. for this assignment, they were not to keep any records on the tribal elders. They could record their conversation to document pertinent information, but they were only there to assess needs and areas where the United States government could assist the locals. It had been impressed upon Nic that if it could be proven that a tribal elder had given up sensitive information, accidently, they and their family could be killed. So, they were to destroy those records once they had the information that they needed.

"I'm sorry, but I was told that we could document the tribal elders and then we were to destroy any sensitive information that night."

"Oh, right, right. I just meant that if we forgot to ask a particular question in a region, we could go back and ask them the questions. We need this information to keep track of where the tribes are, who they are affiliated with, and if they've had any contact with the Taliban, or other insurgents."

"They're not going to tell you shit," Ramirez said.

"Aw." Max looked at Ramirez's nametag. "Sgt. Ramirez, we have things to entice them. We aren't just going to go in there and pepper them with questions. We'll go in and pass out soccer balls to the boys and cookies and tea for the families. Soccer is big here."

"You think a soccer ball is going to get them to let their guard down?"

"That and perhaps other perks for helping out," Drummond said, swinging a circle on his map with a small pencil compass. "I've brought some things with me to help negotiate with the locals."

Ramirez shook her head and mumbled something under her breath. Nic felt the tension simmering with Ramirez. The old saying that a watched pot never boils wouldn't apply to Ramirez; she was about to pop her top and Nic couldn't figure out why.

"I understand we have an interpreter coming

with us," Nic said, watching Ramirez out of the corner of her eye.

"Yes, I was able to procure a local named Ami. Very nice young man, he passed the requisite background check and he's from a university in Kabul. His English is very good." Max measured out a line and then put his pencil and highlighter down. "So, shall we discuss the coming week?"

"We're going to be out a week?" Nic said, writing down some notes.

"Well, we will move to the next FOB, forward operating base," he said, looking at Ramirez as if she needed an explanation.

Great, he was insulting as well as stupid. If he thought he needed to explain every acronym, they were going to be in big trouble.

"I know what FOB is," Ramirez said tersely. "Fucking pencil pusher," she said under her breath. Nic looked at Ramirez and frowned. "Ma'am," Ramirez said, grinding her teeth.

"Continue, Mr. Drummond."

"Well, we will be engaging tribes as we move forward to the next FOB. I figure we can be out for a few days to week at a time. This will keep us moving and able to stay in one area for a little longer if we stay in those locations."

"Where you gonna sleep, Casper?" Ramirez's attitude was a complete about-face from earlier. Frankly, Nic was shocked at her behavior.

"Ramirez."

"Ma'am. Clearly, he hasn't been over here. He has no idea what it's like out there and he thinks he is going to just walk in and talk to people who live on dirt floors and live in constant fear of the terrorists around here. What does he think we're doing here?"

"Ramirez, can I speak to you in private?" Nic stood. "Mr. Drummond, can you excuse us for a moment?"

"Of course, take all the time you need." He went back to a stack of papers, thumbing through them, ignoring them instantly.

"Sergeant, what are you doing?" Nic hovered over Ramirez. She wasn't trying to intimidate Ramirez, but she was pissed. "You haven't said boo all day and now you decide you're gonna jump this civilian? What gives?"

"The guy's a spook. I don't like being used for government bullshit." Ramirez puffed up and looked at Nic. "Ma'am."

"Very unprofessional, Sergeant. You're an NCO, you're a leader, I expected more out of you," Nic said, turning away and sitting back at the table, leaving Ramirez standing alone. She wasn't Ramirez's commander, but she could voice her displeasure at the behavior. Nic noticed the spook comment. There was something about the guy, but she'd already had that feeling. Spook wasn't on her list, but now that Ramirez mentioned it, it was like a boulder in a road, it couldn't be unseen. She'd have to figure out if there was anything to Ramirez's comment, or be able to work around the boulder.

Sitting back down, they spent the next hour working out a series of short trips out into the country. The next few weeks would find them sleeping in the Humvee, as they traversed Afghanistan. Drummond thought he would be able to get lodgings for them, but both Nic and Ramirez agreed that they would sleep in the Humvee. They weren't comfortable taking advantage of the locals, but if it presented itself, Drummond didn't seem to mind. Something was definitely wrong with this, very wrong.

Chapter Thirteen

"How do I look?" Jordan said, twirling around in her new dress.

"Wow. You look fantastic." Claire smiled; her friend had outdone herself this time. She would once again catch every eye in the room. Even the ones with golden bracelets adhered to their fingers.

"Good, I don't want to make you look bad."

"Oh, far from it, sweetie, you're going to get us lots of attention."

"Good. Oh hey, is Tim's mom going to be there?"

"I don't know, why?" Claire looked at Jordan suspiciously.

"Hmm, just wondering." Jordan walked back into the bathroom to finish her makeup.

Claire followed and leaned against the doorjamb. She knew something was frying on the brain of Jordan's and she wanted to know what.

"What gives, Jordan?"

Jordan closed her eye, pushing eyelashes through her mascara brush. Without looking at Claire, she said, "Grace just told me that she likes playing with him, but that maybe she would have to stop because of some things he'd said about you and Nic."

"What did she tell you?"

"Well, she told me that they play guns all the time and that his mommy, or was it his daddy - doesn't matter, it's from the same family—that he said you gals were carpet munchers and that you couldn't get married. He said a few other things that I don't think a six-year-old should say. Disgusting really, but that shit comes from the parents. Kids are just little parrots, repeating what their uneducated parents say. Sad really."

"Look, Nic and I had a conversation with his parents. While I'd like to say it went well, we came to an agreement. Grace wouldn't be allowed to go to their house to play."

"An agreement?"

"Let's just say that Nic made it very clear that our relationship was none of their business and they made it clear that how they raise their son was none of ours. So we agreed that it would be in the best interest of all involved if our children didn't play together. End of discussion."

"I see." Jordan scoffed and then pursed her lips together.

Oh great, this wasn't going to be good thing if Tim's mom was in attendance at the party. She should cancel now, feigning a sudden illness.

"Don't even think about it," Jordan said, pointing the mascara brush in the mirror at Claire.

"What?"

"I know what you're thinking, you're suddenly feeling ill. You're not backing out of this, besides, I promise to be on my best behavior, now that I know you've talked to that future little sociopath. Besides, I mean, you have Nic's career to think about, me – they don't know me from Eve. Maybe I should have a sweet little conversation with her. That's all."

"It's never *that's all*, Jordan." Claire knew once Jordan got something in her head, it was rare that she could talk Jordan out of it. All she could do was stay close to Jordan and not let her off her elbow. That way Jordan wouldn't think of confronting Tim's mom in front of her.

"Oh kitten, relax. It's all good. I don't plan to make a scene. Now, I can't vouch for Tim's mom, but if she's an officer's wife, I suspect she'll keep her cool as well."

"Don't, Jordan, leave it alone. We're going to be moving, so it doesn't matter." Claire hated confrontations like this, it made her squishy.

"Honey, people do this shit because they can. They say crap and then wrap it in God cloth as if God gives them the right to say whatever they disagree with, or if they find it offensive, or that they think is against God's law. I'm calling bullshit on that idea, bullshit." Jordan went back to applying blush to her cheeks. "Now, go get changed and let's get this party started."

"Don't, Jordan, I'm warning you. We've handled it and I don't want anything getting back to Nic in Afghanistan. You know how wives talk."

"I promise, kitten. I won't say a thing," Jordan said, putting away her makeup. "Unless someone says something to me," she mumbled.

"Jordan..."

Jordan crossed her heart and held up three fingers. "Promise."

"Uh huh," Claire said, as she grumbled all the way down the hall. Good thing Grace was at the sitter's, otherwise...well, it was just a good thing.

❧ ❧ ❧ ❧

Cars lined the street and from the looks of it, Claire was going to have to park around the block. Couples holding hands walked down the street; the crisp night was perfect for a party. Too hot and people would be drinking heavily, too cold and it kept the drinking to a minimum until they warmed up. Either way it was a party where alcohol would be in abundant supply. The conversation on the way over had be stilted between Claire and Jordan, neither wanting a confrontation about Tim's mom.

"You look sexy, kitten," Jordan said.

"I wasn't going for sexy, but thank you." Claire patted Jordan's hand. "Truce?"

"Were we fighting?" Jordan grabbed Claire's hand and patted it back. "I just thought we were exchanging ideas. I'm fine, besides I could never be mad at you." She leaned over and kissed Claire on the cheek, just as Tim's wide-eyed mom and dad walked by her window.

"Shit."

"What?"

"There goes Tim's mom and dad. I guess I'm just scandalous. I'm sure I'm now cheating on Nic with you. God, can't I catch a break?

"Screw 'em. Anyone who knows you, knows you're a one-woman-man, I mean woman." Jordan laughed. "Let's get in there before they do and get a drink. We could spread a rumor that we caught them fucking in the car. That'll throw them off and they'll spend the whole party denying the allegation." Jordan cackled at the crude reference.

"Jordan."

"What, it's just a little fun. No big deal."

"Uh huh. Behave." Claire gave her a stern look

and then knocked on the door.

A short rotund woman with perfect hair with a flip, pearls, and a rather snug dress opened the door. "Claire, how are you? Who's your friend?"

"Mrs. Chamberlain, how are you? You're looking wonderful. Have you lost weight?" Claire smeared the flattery around so thick, Mrs. Chamberlain couldn't resist. Besides, Commander Chamberlain was Nic's mentor and the one responsible for her being sent to Afghanistan. So sucking up to the Mrs. would get her points, no matter what was said at the party. "This is my friend that I've known since college, Jordan. Jordan, Mrs. Chamberlain."

"Well, it's a pleasure to meet you." Jordan extended her hand and shook a limp wrist.

"Are you visiting? Where are you from? It's so nice of you to accompany Claire while Nic is overseas. Have you heard from Nic?" Mrs. Chamberlain had barely come up for air before the doorbell rang again. "Oh excuse me, I need to get that, please make yourselves at home. Drinks are out on the patio and fingers are on the kitchen table, out on the patio and…" A soft knock made Mrs. Chamberlain turn without saying another word.

"Boy, does she come up for air or is she breathing out her ass? I think she meant finger foods, but hey I wouldn't put it past her to serve fingers, she seems a little scattered." Jordan tucked her clutch under her arm and scooped up a plate, napkin, and then cruised the finger foods, filling her plate past what was acceptable. Claire shot her a look, but she only shrugged and smiled around an olive. "I'm hungry."

"Obviously."

"Oh shit," Claire said, looking across the room.

"What?"

"Hmm, nothing," she said, turning back to the finger foods. "Let's head out to the patio and see what they have to drink. I think I need a double."

"Now you're talking my language. Lead the way, Captain Obvious."

"What's that supposed to mean?"

"I'm assuming that you caught a glimpse of Tim's mom and dad." Jordan looked back through the panes of glass into the house and pointed at Tim's parents. They were taking to a guy that could have passed for an old John Wayne. He was cut right out of a forties movie with his crew cut, shirt with a tie, and button down sweater. His razor sharp creases on his khaki pants and loafers completed the look. "Hey, who's that talking to Tim's parents?"

"The commandant that sent Nic to Afghanistan." Claire didn't need to look; she'd seen him earlier, tapping a pipe against his palm.

"Geez, he looks like he's time warped from a John Wayne movie. The only thing missing is a swagger. Wait, wait, naw, he walks like he's got sh-"

"Jordan. Stop." Claire ordered a drink from the bartender working the bar. "Here." She passed Jordan a glass of wine.

"Thanks, I've got a bead on mom, she's coming this way," Jordan said, with a tad too much glee in her voice. The only thing missing was a group of girls chanting fight, fight, fight.

"Claire, there you are, I've been looking all over for you. How are you? How's Nic? I heard she was shipped over to Afghanistan, tragic. Just graduated and all." Turning towards Jordan, she flashed her brightest smile. "And who do we have here?"

Jordan thrust her hand out. "Jordan. Do I detect a southern accent? Mississippi?"

"Oh my gosh, I thought I'd gotten rid of it with all the travel we've done in the last ten years. Alabama. Have you been?"

"Well, that explains so much. Bless your heart, you are southern through and through, aren't you?" Jordan just beamed, waiting to pounce. "Mrs.?"

"Oh, where are my manners? You can call me Jane."

"Jane, it's a pleasure to meet you. Aren't you little Tim's mom?"

"Oh, have you met Tim? He is just a chip off the ol' block. Just like his dad over there." Jane pointed to Tim Sr.

"Well, no, I haven't had the pleasure to meet Tim, but Grace has told me so much about him." Jordan threaded her arm through Jane's and smiled so wide Claire was afraid she'd break something. "By the way, did you know Claire and Nic just got married?"

Several beats of silence threaded its way between the three women before Jane uncomfortably said, "No, I didn't know. Well, that's wonderful. Congratulations, Claire."

"You must be surprised that Nic and Claire could get married. I mean Tim said that you told him carpet munchers couldn't get married. That is how you referred to Nic and Claire, wasn't it?"

"Excuse me?"

"Well, the apple doesn't fall far from the tree, so I assume that's the kind of language you use around your son. Grace doesn't need to hear something so nasty about her moms; you really should watch your tongue before someone rips it out at the root. It'd be a shame if someone thought you and your husband were homophobic and it would be an even bigger shame if that got back to his commander. I mean, I'm sure you'd never meant to refer to Claire as something as nasty as a carpet muncher. Did you?" Jordan didn't take a breath as she landed verbal blow after verbal blow. Claire pinched the back of her arm and she finally stopped. Turning towards Claire, she flashed a quick smile and then looked at Jane.

Jane turned three shades of red. Not from embarrassment; clearly she wasn't classy enough to be embarrassed. Claire assumed it was from being confronted at a party where Jane didn't have an egress route. Women like Jane weren't usually used to being called out for their behavior. The wives gossiped and talked so nasty about people, Claire wondered if they knew they talked about each other the same way. Drama.

"Jordan, we should go," Claire said quietly, her back to Jane.

"Just a minute, kitten. You know, I heard a funny story the other day when I was at the bank. Seems some people can't keep their business private, or their personal life personal. Did you hear this story, Claire?"

"I'm not sure what story you're referring to, Jordan."

"Well, here, let me tell it to you. You are going to love this, Jane. Stop me if you've heard this story." Jordan scooted closer to Jane and swished her straw through her drink. "I had to make a quick stop at the bank the other day, bank error or something, and I just realized I saw one of the wives here at the party at that very bank. Seems she was standing in line waiting for the next teller with her son. When he started acting up, she tried to correct him..." Jordan suddenly had a thick southern accent like Jane's and she hung on the word *him*, long enough to see Jane turn an ashen color. "When she jerked his little body around and said something in his ear, the little guy blurted out, 'If you spank me, I'll tell daddy I saw some guy's peepee in your mouth.'" Jordan looked across the room, a smug smiled planted firmly across her face.

"Then what happened?" Claire was shocked at the revelation and started to eye each of the wives at the party. She wasn't surprised, cheating wasn't uncommon amongst the wives, but she was shocked that someone's son had witness the indiscretion.

"Well, that's the funny part. I don't know. *Mom* jerked his arm right up and marched him out of the bank." Jordan looked at Jane and waited.

"Oh geez, Jordan, don't repeat that story. That could hurt someone's marriage and we shouldn't jump to conclusions," Claire said, trying to be polite and just loud enough for Jane and Jordan's ears.

"Yes, something like that could be very hurtful, couldn't it? Like calling two women who love each other carpet munchers, or saying that they don't have the right to get married, that it's against God's law." Jordan turned to Jane, who suddenly looked sick. "Isn't that right, Jane? We really should watch what we say and do around our children. They aren't born to hate, they learn that at home. They are little sponges, soaking up everything around them. Wouldn't you agree?"

Jane's lips moved but nothing came out. Her gaze darted around the room, looking to see who was within earshot of the story Jordan just relayed. Clutching her stomach, she politely excused herself. "I'm sorry, I need to use the rest room. If you ladies will excuse me. It was wonderful to see you again, Claire, pleasure to meet you, Jordan. Have a wonderful evening."

Jane rushed through the sliders and into the house. Where, Claire wasn't sure, but something told her that Jordan had just put Jane in her place.

"Who did you see at the bank?" Claire questioned.

"Isn't it obvious?"

"Jane?"

"Hmm, I doubt little Tim will be making any more trips to the bank with his mommy. Good thing you and Nic decided he wasn't playmate material, probably for the best anyway. Riff-raff like that doesn't need to be around our little princess. Now where are those tasty little finger sandwiches?"

"Oh my God, why didn't you tell me you saw Jane at the bank?"

"Didn't know it was Jane," Jordan said around a sandwich tucked in her cheek. "Besides, when I saw her tonight I was just going to ignore her. I figure she didn't see me standing there listening to the whole thing." Jordan laid her hand on Claire's arm and said, "Could you imagine if I had a kid and they slipped into my bedroom? That poor child would need therapy for the rest of her life." Jordan shivered. "Just creeps me out thinking about what Tim saw, so no playing with Tim. He is way older than his little six years, girl."

Claire thought about what Jordan just said. Did she need to have a talk with Grace about Tim? They had spent a lot of time playing in the backyard and at his house. Her stomach dropped at the thought. She wanted to bolt and just as she was about to say something to Jordan, she stopped Claire.

"I've already talked to Grace, honey. Nothing happened between them. When I saw him at the house that was my first thought too. So, Grace and I had tea and talked about stuff."

"What kind of stuff?"

"You know, the kind of stuff that aunties and their favorite nieces talk about. Guns, zombies, boys, girls, touching, the usual."

"She didn't say anything?" Claire worried Grace was too young to have that kind of talk.

"Nope, and trust me, I know how to grill someone about their sex life."

"She's six, she doesn't have a sex life." Claire wanted to smack Jordan.

"Of course she doesn't. Heck, she doesn't even like boys. Which is a good thing, with all this facebook and twitter and chat stuff going around. Did I tell you I saw a group of kindergarteners sitting in front of the school texting?" Jordan stuffed another sandwich in her mouth. "I asked them who they could possibly be texting and do you know what they said?"

Claire shook her head, still too freaked out about the whole Tim situation.

"One of them gave me a look like I was stupid and said, 'we're texting each other.'"

"Are you serious?"

"I wish I wasn't. I wanted to rip those phones right out of those little stubby hands and throw them in the trash, but I'm sure someone's mommy would have come looking for me. Can you believe that?"

"They grow up too quick, Jordan. Too quick."

"They don't have to, but now it's a tether to the helicopter moms. They can keep an eye, or ear on them anywhere, anytime."

"I'm not letting Grace out of the house until she's forty. By then Nic and I will be in a retirement home, with dementia, and won't give a damn."

"Oh calm down, you and Nic are doing just fine. She doesn't have her own computer, or iPad and anything like that, so you're safe, so far."

Claire didn't feel any safer. Grace had been asking for all of those things and Nic's leaving almost had Claire give in.

"Come on, pumpkin. Let's go see what trouble we can stir up." Jordan had a little smirk that told Claire it might be time to go home.

"We should probably go, you've caused enough damage. Besides, it's getting late."

"We just got here."

"I'll make our apologies, you get the coats," Claire ordered.

"Okay."

"No stops along the way there, Ms. 'stop me if you've heard this story.'"

Jordan only smiled and waved at Claire. God, just let them make it to the car without an incident. Please.

Chapter Fourteen

The tepid water ran down Nic's body, washing off what she was sure was a pound of sand and dirt. Sand was everywhere – her bunk, her clothes, she even wiped down a fine layer from her photographs every day. The worst was the food. The gritty taste was enough to make her pack MREs and eat 'em in her CHU, if it wasn't for the fact that her air conditioning unit seemed to be the reason for the fine layer all over her stuff. As far as the food was concerned, it was probably all in her head, but every time she took a bite, all she thought she tasted was sand.

Not wanting to waste the over filled hand of shampoo, Nic lathering her head, scrubbing down to the scalp. The piles of bubbles started to cascade down her body when she heard someone clear their throat.

"Sorry, I didn't know someone was in here. You forgot to lock the door," Ramirez said.

"Oh shit. No problem. Sorry, the other showers were out of order, so I thought I would use these. I didn't mean to screw up anyone's routine or anything. Just give me a minute and I'll be out of your hair."

"Pun intended," Ramirez said caustically.

"Yeah, sorry."

"No problem, Colonel, I'll just wait outside."

"Thanks, I'm almost done." Nic flipped the handle and jumped as cold water assaulted her body.

While it might be hot in the desert, she still loved a hot shower. She was weird like that, she supposed. She was already perspiring as she slipped her shorts on and flung her towel over her shoulder. God, she hated the desert heat.

"All yours." Nic tossed her thumb at the door.

Ramirez looked at Nic and then started to say something, but stopped.

"What's on your mind, Sergeant?" Nic could read people, well, most people. Ramirez was still a mystery novel that she couldn't figure out the whodunnit part.

Ramirez nodded toward Nic's back and stammered, "I couldn't help but notice you've got a pretty wicked scar. Do you mind if I ask how you got it?"

Nic's brow furrowed. "I think you already did?"

"Yeah, I guess I did. You don't have to answer if you don't want. I get it." Ramirez grabbed her toiletry bag and started walking towards the shower.

"I was in an accident in Iraq," Nic blurted out, wondering why she felt compelled to tell Ramirez. She wasn't ashamed of the scar. It had been her penance for surviving the helicopter crash that killed her whole crew. "Why do you want to know?"

Ramirez did a slow turn towards Nic, raising her battle shirt, exposing her own disfigured back. The deep fragmented skin had the telltale signs of a burn. A long scar bisected her back, its raised edge remnants of a surgical scalpel.

Now Nic understood Ramirez's attitude, her demeanor, why she was less approachable than a camel spider. She carried the wounds of a soldier who'd seen combat, but she was only guessing. Looking for confirmation, she searched Ramirez's stoic gaze. Was she a comrade in arms?

"What happened?" She questioned.

Ramirez looked away, towards the jagged mountain range and then back at Nic. "I was part of a squad assigned to a visiting senator. He wanted to get out and see the country. Tour the FOBs and press the flesh. Told us he was here on a listening tour, talk to the service members, and get a feeling for what the war was doing to the locals." Ramirez was pulling a thread from her towel, unraveling it as she told her story and then suddenly she stopped.

Silence pressed between them as Nic waited for a cue from Ramirez. Stories like Nic's weren't rare, but she'd never met another female who'd had similar injuries. Sure, she'd seen a few at the hospital in D.C when she was shipped back, but she'd been in her own world of hurt and pain.

"I'm sorry." Nic clapped Ramirez's shoulder and gently squeezed.

Ramirez let a soft chuckle slip past her lips and wiped her eyes. "Why? You didn't do this to me, ma'am."

"No, but I think I have a pretty good idea what you went through."

"You got hit by a TOW missile too?"

"Jesus, you got hit by a missile? Christ." Nic sunk against the wall and sighed.

"Yep, the hummer I was in was the first in a line of vehicles traipsing out on the country side, so a D.C. type could look important back home."

Max Drummond hit a nerve for Ramirez. He was as D.C. as they came, so Nic understood why Ramirez was defiant when Drummond casually talked about a jaunt out beyond the walls of Camp Leatherneck. Ramirez would be right back out where she was when a missile hit her convoy.

"What are you doing here? Even the Army isn't heartless when it comes to combat injuries."

"My team was being redeployed and I wanted to be with my unit."

Nic shook her head. What was home life like if she picked this over being home safe and sound?

"Wow, I'm not sure I know what to say, Sergeant."

"I need the paycheck, Colonel. So there's nothing to say. I have a mouth to feed back home and for now, I'm good at what I do. I like being a soldier; I love my brothers in my unit and I'd do anything for them. This," Ramirez said, pointing to her back. "It comes with the job."

Nic knew the feeling of loving the people you worked with, she loved her crew. That's why it tore her up that she survived and they didn't. But she still felt like they died for the wrong reasons and it was her fault they were dead. Nic would carry that with her until they played Taps for her.

"What happened to you?" Ramirez asked.

Now it was Nic's turn to bare her soul if she wanted, to relive her near-death experience. She rarely shared her combat injury, except when she had her yearly physical. The dialogue was always the same – Does it hurt? You need to keep stretching or the scar will tighten. Are you exercising? Blah, blah, blah, she knew the routine by heart and was always ready with the same answers.

"My helicopter was hit by a missile, I was thrown clear, but my crew was killed." Sweat peppered Nic's face as she remembered the explosion and waking up in a hospital in Germany. A tremor started in her hands and worked its way through her body. Clamping her hands together, she pushed through the memory. She wouldn't let anyone see her weakness. Her PTSD had been manageable in the past, but she hadn't been in a combat zone since Iraq. Now talking to Ramirez, the memories rushed back, her system flooded with anxiety. A strange sensation, but not foreign to her.

"You were a helicopter pilot?"

"Yep."

"We didn't lose anyone, but that bastard from D.C. turned tail and ran home before we could even get the wounded on a transport to Germany."

Ramirez talked as if she wasn't one of the wounded.

"How many were wounded?"

"Everyone in my hummer and the hummer behind me." Ramirez ticked off each soldier on her fingers, giving each a name. "I'm sorry about your crew," she said, still pulling at the now frayed end of her towel.

They had a connection. They shared a similar experience regardless of rank or service, that linked them in that weird way victims of violence were united. It explained a lot about Ramirez, who she was, why she acted the way she did, and moving forward, Nic suspected that something would be different between them, but then again maybe she was just projecting her feelings on Ramirez. Suddenly a phantom pain coursed through her body. She hadn't had one in a year and now she could feel another start to spike and slice through her back, through the scar tissue. PTSD was a wicked bitch that showed no one mercy, no one.

"Well, I should get back to my CHU. I have

some paperwork I need to take care of. Have a good evening, Ramirez. I'll see you in the morning."

All she wanted to do was run, run until her legs couldn't carry her anymore. Run until the faces of her crew buried themselves back in the far reaches of her memory. She'd seen them every night for months after her accident and now she knew they would visit her again in her dreams. Pleading to save them, reaching for her like they had for months. Not even a priest would be able to exorcise her demons and she'd left Father O'Reilly back at Camp Pendleton when she'd left for NPS.

"Have a good evening, Colonel."

"You do the same, Sergeant."

Nic started to jog away from her CHU and towards the wall, her demons propelling her faster. Stretching her legs, she cleared a few obstacles that piled up around the wall. Mostly empty boxes, they weren't worth anything and if stolen, the thieves wouldn't get anything. The soldiers had strict order to keep everything away from the walls, for fear of being stolen. She weaved her way around CHUs, the motor pool, and some makeshift hammocks slung between trucks. The heat made some men sleep outdoors where there was at least a breeze and they could keep an eye on their equipment. Combat was different and sometimes protocol be damned. They all had to survive and to survive you had to live the best way one could, faced with these wretched conditions.

Her mind drifted to a group of men playing soccer. She'd seen boys kicking balls outside the walls of the base. From her understanding, the military had provided tons of soccer balls to the locals. They called it an investment in morale; interesting investment, she thought.

Sweat poured down her T-shirt as she pushed harder. Her joints screamed at her, but she screamed back at them. She wasn't going to relent. They'd called her out with the phantom pains, so she would give them something to complain about tomorrow. Another motor pool hummed with laughter, the sounds of metal on metal, and music. A deep voice yelled at her.

"Hey, what are you running from?"

"Maybe someone's chasing her?"

"Hey gorgeous, why don't you come over here and we can give you a work out."

A raucous laughter broke out as a few men slapped each other on the back. She slowed down and peered into the overly bright covering.

"Is that how you talk to the women on this base?" she said to no one in particular.

Waiting for an answer, she walked into the light and looked each man in the face. The men ranged anywhere from twenty to fifty, she'd guess. They were from all different nationalities and none of them had a complete uniform on. Stripped down to their camos and boots, their bodies wore the marks of their tribes, tattoos. Girlfriends, kids, tribal marks, colorful paintings that could have hung on walls in peoples home, all adorned most of the arms, backs, and chests. The artwork on one soldier's chest laid testament to those in his unit that had died. Three sets of boots, rifles, and helmets resting on the butt of the rifle laying over his heart. The universal symbol for a lost life was easy to recognize and respect.

"Who wants to know?" Someone from the back said.

"No one in particular," she said, locking eyes with each man. None flinched away from her gaze, so she knew she was better off leaving them to their own devices. "Have a good evening, men," she said in her most commanding voice. "I'm sure I'll see you around." It almost sounded like a threat and that's how she wanted to leave it.

Sprinting out of the lean-to, she heard someone say, "Who the hell was that?"

"Got me, but did you see that ass? What I would do for a piece of…"

She let the sounds of her thumping feet on the sand drown out their voices and snide comments. Tomorrow she'd get her first chance to encounter the local tribal elders as they moved toward their first FOB. She had a feeling a good night's sleep would elude her, but maybe she'd catch Claire on Skype. If not, she'd send her an email with her itinerary for the next week and when to she could expect to hear from Nic.

Turning towards her CHU, she slowed down to a walk and let her mind wander to Claire and what she might be doing right about now.

Chapter Fifteen

Claire stood at the edge of the room, waiting and watching how the wives sat on one side and the men stood either off on the other side or outside, a few smoking. Small gaggles of three or four men chatted and then one would leave and work their way to the group with the commander in it. Each man who approached shook his hand, said something that made the commander and the group laugh and then he was allowed to step into the group and join in, usually causing one of the other men to leave and get a drink, find his wife, whisper in her ear, and then join the group who lost a member.

Claire had never really paid that much attention to how the men worked the room. She never had to. Nic was always with her and together they worked the room, talking to those they knew and avoiding those who were more trouble than they were worth. Claire stared at the commander. He was the reason Nic was in Afghanistan, but protocol prevented her from confronting him and calling him out on his misdeed. She wanted to, she wanted to go up and slap the stupid grin he shared with the other dolts laughing and joking while her wife was sent into a combat zone.

No, she was an officer's wife and she needed to control her emotions. Some people looked at the commander like God, his word was law. No matter how bad the law was, it was still followed. One day she would tell the commander's wife what she thought of him.

"There you are." Jordan threaded her arm through Claire's and wrapped her arm around her thin waste. "You need a cookie, maybe a whole pack. So who we starin' at?" Jordan inquired at the new game being played.

"I'm not staring, Jordan."

"No, you're plotting and I want to help."

"I'm not plotting, I'm waiting for you." She held up their wraps as evidence. "See."

Jordan scanned the room, looking around. "Where's Jane? I want to say goodbye."

"Oh, no, you don't, we're leaving and I'm not going to put her through another encounter of *guess who we saw today*. So, let's go say our goodbyes to the hostess and be on our way." Claire ushered Jordan towards Mrs. Chamberlain.

"Aw, you're no fun."

"No, I'm not. I'll probably have to see these ladies again and I don't want tongues wagging later." Claire worked her way to their hostess and smiled. "Mrs. Chamberlain, thank you for a lovely evening."

"Going so soon, Claire?" Mrs. Chamberlain reached for Claire's hand and cradled it between her own plump ones.

"Yes, I'm afraid it's a school night and I need to get home. Thank you again for inviting us."

"Well, it was my pleasure and it was wonderful meeting you, Jordan. I hope we didn't bore you tonight," she said, releasing Claire's hand and shaking Jordan's.

"No, not at all. In fact, I find military wives are wonderful to talk to, selfless in their devotion to their husband and children and so giving to the community. Just this evening I was talking to Jane and her—"

"Oh my, would you look at the time? I've got to get to the sitter's before ten. I'm sorry, Jordan, we need to go."

"Of course. It was a pleasure to meet you, Mrs. Chamberlain."

Claire practically pushed Jordan out the door and down the steps.

"What the hell?" she said, pulling on Jordan's arm. "You were going to—"

"What?" Jordan pulled her wrap around her shoulders and smiled wickedly.

"God, I can't take you anywhere, can I?"

Chapter Sixteen

One month after deployment

Sunlight streamed through the fragile curtains, if you could even call them curtains, offering no relief from the heat of the morning. Nic threw an arm over her eyes, hoping for just a few more minutes of much needed sleep. Perhaps if she wished for it, she'd see Claire again. If she tried really hard, she might even have a moment of skin-on-skin contact. Her lover hovered above her, taunting her. Claire's breasts gently swung towards her as she leaned in for a kiss.

"Hmm, morning comes way too early, lover," Claire said between kisses. Her soft lips tempted Nic to stay in bed just a few more minutes longer.

Nic reached up and grasped Claire's soft breasts, running her thumb across nipples that were in a constant state of excitement. Pinching them gently, she pulled the tips and squeezed. Claire arched into her hands, letting a soft moan escape her lips. Grabbing Nic's hands, she pulled them tightly against her breasts and smiled down at Nic.

"So it's going to be one of those mornings, is it?"

"Baby, if I had my way, every morning would be one of those mornings."

Nic released her hold, wrapped her arms around Claire, and flipped her onto her back. Grinding her hips into Claire, she felt herself start to get wet, but the sheets between them kept her from feeling Claire's own wetness. God, she loved the way Claire worked her. She had a way of seducing Nic, even when it was hotter than hell and everything stuck together, including skin.

Bang, bang, bang, sprung Nic from her dream. "Fuck."

"Colonel Caldwell, the bird wants to see you on deck."

Fuck, back to reality, Nic thought, throwing her legs over her rack. It was probably just as well, if she got too much further, she might find a glimpse of happiness in this shit hole. One month and she still wasn't used to finding sand everywhere. Grabbing a bag of wet wipes, she started her daily routine of cleaning up. Running water was a commodity that was in short supply and since their last delivery was bombed on its way to camp, they were rationing what they had for food and essentials. This beat the last few weeks of sleeping in the hummer out in the tribal lands.

She spent her days with an interpreter, meeting tribal leaders, taking down their information and trying to figure out what they needed, who they knew, and what they knew. It wasn't an easy job to get to the leader, let alone get them to talk to her. First—she was a woman, second—she was part of the U.S. military and lately the military was more hated than the Taliban. If a tribal leader was seen talking to the military, it could go bad for him, but if he did talk to them, he could get something for it. At least that's what they were telling the tribal leaders. She also passed out soccer balls to the kids, had tea with the men, and stayed as far away from the women as possible.

"Hey Colonel, did you hear me?"

"Yes, Corporal, I heard you. Please tell Colonel Jess I'm on my way."

"Yes, ma'am."

Looking down at her uniform, she groaned. She had one clean one left and she was saving it for her trip home in a few weeks. Picking up the one she wore yesterday, she opened the door to her shack and flicked it one more time to get the dust off it. She shook her head. God, she was retiring after this assignment. Claire had been understanding when she'd come down on orders to mobilize to Afghanistan, but Nic knew Claire worried. Nic was sure it was hard not to; Claire had lost so much the last time someone was deployed. Three years had gone by so fast, and they were just starting to build their relationship, get settled, build a life for Claire and Grace, and finish her degree. God, she wished she was home now.

O-six-hundred was late for desert duty. The heat would be brutal today. Grabbing her Shemagh head wrap, she groaned as she wrapped it around her neck and grabbed her cover. She'd need the scarf to replace her hat if she was going out into the countryside with her civilian counterpart and the interpreter. Dust storms were predicted for today and the Shemagh would keep the dust out of her nose and eyes. She'd had a constant sore throat from trying to clear it from the desert dirt, since arriving. Hoisting her IMTV, Improved Modular Tactical Vest, over her head, she groaned as she lashed it to her body. She'd be sweating before she left her shack with no relief in sight until she got back after her mission. Pulling her sidearm from its holster on her chest, she popped the clip, double checked it, and thrust it back into its home. Slipping her three-point sling over her shoulder, she rotated her M4 and settled in to it. Then she rotated it around, pointing it down while she finished her equipment assessment. Tapping her ammo pouches and webbing, she made sure she had all her gear. Now she knew why they called it "battle rattle". Every time she walked, something rattled on her, from the sloshing in her canteen, to the ammo pouches. She was a far cry from her days flying a helicopter where most times she wore a vest and a sidearm with her helmet.

Grabbing her note pad, she sat on her cot, flipped past a few pages and jotted down some notes. She read them over again and added something else before closing it up and tucking it in the side pocket on her uniform.

Thinking about their mission for the next few days, Nic sighed. Their interviews hadn't gone as well as Max Drummond, the civilian she was working with, had hoped. The Afghan people were guarded and they had every right to be skeptical of what they were trying to do. Hell, she was skeptical. She'd had more tea with tribal elders, and passed out more soccer balls to the kids trying to open doors, only to have those doors slammed in their face. It didn't matter; she was undeterred. Nic had a job to do and she wanted to get home to Claire, so the sooner they had the information D.C. needed, she'd be on a military transport home and out of this hellhole.

Looking at her watch, she double checked it, noted the time, then grabbed her duffle. Today they were going to a province a day's ride away, which meant she'd be sleeping in the Humvee for the next couple of days. Nights in the desert could drop so low a person would wonder if it was really August or the middle of winter. If she wasn't careful she would miss her Skype time with Claire; it was her lifeline. It kept her connected to their relationship; it was what helped her put her boots on the ground in the morning and moving forward, one foot in front of the other. As she pushed through the door, the heat assaulted her instantly. Perspiration popped all over her body. Now to see what the colonel wanted.

Pop, pop, pop.

Nic startled when she heard shots fired. It wasn't uncommon to hear gunfire, but these were closer than usual, followed by shouting. She started for the command center, passing a few men in various stages of dress, shaving, working out, or just sitting with ear buds stuck in their ears oblivious to the world.

"What the hell?" she muttered, running in tandem with another soldier.

Looking at the kid, she recognized him from the plane.

"Swicatowski, right?"

"Yes, ma'am. Good memory." He smiled a cocky smile. He was probably thinking he'd left such a good impression that he couldn't be forgotten. "Blue on green, ma'am?" he said, crouching behind a stack of pallets.

"Shit." Nic poked her head over the top of the pallets and ducked back down when more shots echoed through the camp. "Well, if someone was eating their rifle it would be one and done."

Blue on green meant that an Afghanistan soldier or civilian, someone considered a friendly, was shooting at U.S. military. Afghanistan civilians and soldiers, once cleared, were often in the compound.

The U.S. trained them, worked with them, getting them ready to take over from U.S. forces. Some of the civilians were day laborers, and interpreters, indispensable in Nic's line of work, and suddenly she wondered if Ami had reported for work today.

Silence.

Poking her head up again, Nic couldn't see anything moving. Crouching still, she motioned for the soldier next to her to go around the opposite side of the pallet stack. Nic shuffled low towards the door of HQ. Hugging the wall, she peeked around the corner and then jerked her head back. A quick look and her gaze lit on two soldiers lying in a pool of blood and another soldier was sitting on the floor, leaning against the wall, clutching his chest. A stampede of feet pulled her attention away and toward three men running towards her with their weapons drawn and aiming at her. Standing, Nic's hand rose, signaling the men to stop.

"What's the situation, Colonel?" an Army staff sergeant asked.

"Two soldiers on the floor, on leaning against the wall, and I can't see anything anyone else."

"We'll take it from here, Colonel."

Nic turned towards the sergeant and frowned.

"Sergeant."

"Colonel, I don't have time to argue with you," he said, throwing hand signals and silently moving towards the entrance. Before she could say anything, he was inside stepping over the bodies and down the hallway. She watched as the squad covered each other, split into two groups, and disappeared out of sight.

"Lieutenant Colonel, what do we do now?"

"Stand down," she commanded.

Josh squatted across from her, barely twenty if he was lucky. His face looked like it had never seen a razor, fuzz barely sprouting on his cheeks. She could hear his gun rattle as he shook in nervous anticipation. He'd probably see more combat action in his young life than most soldiers would see in their whole military careers. Six months from now, he'd age a lifetime and that fresh faced kid from small town America would be a combat hardened man. She shook her head, remembering her own crew from Iraq and her young crew chief who had died too young, leaving behind a wife and baby.

More shots rang out from inside HQ. Nic looked back into the building when suddenly the window behind her exploded. Nic shielded her face from the flying glass as a man in an Afghanistan uniform fell to the ground, trying to maintain his grasp on his M16. Twisting, Nic raised her M4 and aimed it at the man. As more shots rang out deeper in the building behind her, Nic's laser focus stayed on the groaning man as he tried to move.

"Don't move," she yelled. Pushing closer, she kicked the M16 away from him. His reach followed the sliding rifle, so Nic stepped on his hand. Josh ran over and put the muzzle of his rifle against the man's head.

"Didn't you hear the Lieutenant Colonel? Don't fucking move," he said, his voice cracking with fear.

Nic started to say something to Josh, but all hell broke loose as the doors to headquarters were pushed open, the metal protesting as they bounced off the cement block walls. The sergeant dumped a man unceremoniously on the ground next to his buddy.

"Medic, where the fuck is a medic?"

A team ran towards them, but as they reached the men on the ground the sergeant said, "Inside, don't worry about these bastards. You treat our men first. These assholes can wait. Cuff 'em."

"You okay?" Nic said, expecting a gruff response. She wasn't disappointed.

"Hell of a lot better than those two in there. God damn assholes, anyone know who these two are?"

He looked around at the crowd that had formed, but no one said anything. Controlled chaos was the order as men ran towards HQ, and out carrying two wounded towards the hospital. Suddenly her civilian counterpart was standing in front of her.

"What happened?" Max Drummond said. His wide-eye stare at the men on the ground was followed by a retching sound as he dashed behind the pallets and expelled his breakfast.

"Guess he's never seen blood before?" Josh said, peering at the pallets.

"No, I don't suppose he has," Nic said, lowering her muzzle and twisting the sling around so the M4 was pointing down. "I'll guess you don't need me, Sergeant, so I'll go and check on my civilian. See you later, Corporal. By the way, get some clothes on, Marine, you're damn near naked out here."

"Yes, ma'am." He started to salute, but she gave him a look that stopped him in mid-salute.

"Lieutenant Colonel, I'm going to need you to write up what you saw out here," the Army sergeant yelled at her back as she rounded the pallets. Max was still hunched over dry heaving when she slapped him on the back.

"You okay?"

He only nodded and waved her off.

"First time seeing that much blood?"

He nodded again.

"Well, if you stay here long enough, you'll probably see it again. So get used to it." She slapped him on the back again and yanked him up. "Let's get you some coffee. We have a couple of tribal elders to see today and I don't want to stay in this shit hole any longer than I have too."

"Was that…was that a dead body in there?" He was more ashen than usual. Desk duty hadn't done him any favors, but his time in the Afghan desert would add some color to his cheeks.

"Yep."

"Oh God," he said, hunching over and puking again.

"Geez, Max. You sure you're ready for this assignment?" She wondered now if he knew what he was getting himself into when he signed up for this job. Or if he had been sold a load of horseshit by his superiors. Didn't matter, they had a job to do and he wasn't going home before she was, so there was only one thing to do, get 'er done.

Chapter Seventeen

Present

"Well, kitten, I say we go out on the town tonight." Jordan sat on the edge of the toilet, chatting away with Claire.

"That sounds wonderful, but there is one little six-year-old issue, Jordie." Claire stood under the jets and tried to relax, but she just had a feeling she needed to stay home tonight. "Not that spending time watching you cruise women isn't fun and all, but Grace just might cock-block any chance of you getting laid tonight. Besides, she's a little young for the bar scene, don't you think?" Claire had been under the water long enough and it wasn't changing her mood. Twisting the shower off, she peeked from behind the shower curtain and thrust out her hand. "Towel please."

"It's probably just as well. I don't think there's a gay bar in this little stretch of beach anyway."

Before Claire could correct Jordan, the doorbell rang.

"Oh, can you get that before it wakes up Grace?"

"Sure thing," Jordan tossed Claire a towel. "Coming," Jordan yelled, walking down the hall.

"Good thing I don't have to worry about the doorbell waking Grace, Jordan can do it all by herself."

Claire's didn't need to wipe the fog off the mirror

to know the stress of Nic being gone was showing. The dark circles weren't a good look for anyone, especially Claire's pale complexion. The sleepless nights were almost too much to bear and she considered seeing her doctor for something to help with the insomnia, but if Nic got a free moment to call, she wanted to be able to rouse from sleeping, and not sound like some stumbling drunk. Then there was Grace to think about. Claire had heard the nightmares of the leading sleep medication and a six-year-old had a way of getting into things when she was being watched like a hawk. Not bad things, but Claire constantly reminded herself of the time Grace had snuck into her makeup bag. She had to admit that fifteen dollars' worth of ruby red lipstick didn't look as good on a six year old as it did on the cat.

Slipping her sweats on, she twisted a towel around her head and passed on one last look in the mirror.

Suddenly, she remembered someone had rung the doorbell and Jordan wasn't back yet. Company? Maybe it was Tim's mom coming to her senses about their argument over the statement *carpet muncher*. Doubtful, but there was always hope for some people that they would come around and see the err of their ways. Claire peeked in on Grace, who still slept, clutching her old stuffed bear Nic had brought her the year they'd meet. Perfect, she was sleeping like an angel, well, an angel with budding horns. Quietly, she shut the door and made her way to the front door.

"Who was at the door, Jor—" Claire felt her knees weaken the minute she saw the two men in uniform standing in the entryway. Grabbing the wall to keep herself from falling, the two men ran over and each grabbed her arms. "Not again."

"Ma'am?" said the one wearing a Chaplain's insignia. "Let's get her over to the sofa."

"Claire, honey...here, drink this." Jordan nervously thrust a glass in her hands. Why would she want something to drink? She wasn't thirsty, she thought.

She could feel tears budding. Staring down at the glass in her hands, she couldn't bring herself to look at the two men. If she ignored them, maybe they would go away and take their bad news with them. This wasn't happening, she couldn't handle losing Nic. What would she tell Grace, again? Oh God, what had she done to deserve so much pain?

"Ma'am, are you Claire Monroe?"

Claire shook her head. Couldn't they just go away and leave them alone? Didn't they know she'd already given one person to the Marine Corps? Did they need to take another?

"Ma'am, my records say that a Claire Monroe lives here—"

"I'm Claire Monroe," she squeaked out, tears rushing down her face.

The couch sagged as Jordan sat next to her, wrapping her arms around Claire. "It'll be okay, kitten."

"No, it won't, not this time, Jordie." Claire wiped at her face, smearing tears across her cheeks. "Nic isn't coming home, is she, Father?"

"Ma'am?"

"My partner, Nichole Caldwell, she isn't coming home, is she?" Claire's voice strengthened with each word.

"Well—"

"When can I expect her body to come home?"

The Chaplain tugged at his collar and looked at the Captain standing next to him. Claire's gaze darted between the two men. Oh God, there aren't any remains to be shipped home. Claire finally lost it as she thought of her lover never coming home at all. She couldn't hold back the tears; dropping her face into her hands, she began to sob uncontrollably. Oh God, how could she go through this again?

Why Nic, don't you have other people to fuck with, God? Haven't I given enough, what more can I give?

Jordan held Claire tighter and rocked her back and forth. "We'll get through this, Claire. We'll get through this," Jordan said, stroking Claire's hair.

"Ma'am, Lt. Colonel Caldwell isn't dead." The Chaplain knelt in front of Claire and put a hand on her shoulder. "She's been injured, but I've been told the prognosis is promising."

"What? She's not dead? What happened? Where is she?" Claire stood and shook out her hands as panic set in. Nic wasn't dead, oh thank God. "Where is she? I need to go to her."

Jordan stopped Claire from pacing and gently said, "Claire, let's find out what the Chaplain has to say and then we can ask questions. Okay?"

"Right. No, you're right, we need more information. How is she? What happened? How badly is she hurt?"

"Ma'am, why don't you sit down and we can tell you what we've been briefed on." The Chaplain pointed to the sofa as he sat on the edge of the recliner.

"Of course, please tell me what you know." Claire was pumped full of adrenaline, her body shook, and she rocked back and forth, waiting. She needed to get to Nic, and the only way she could do that was to find out where she was. Without thinking, she wiped her nose on her sleeve and then swiped at the tears still streaming down her face.

Nic was alive, but hurt. Oh God, she's hurt.

"There was an explosion—"

"An explosion, oh God, this is bad, isn't it?" Turning towards Jordan, she said it again. "This is bad, isn't it?"

"Let's listen to what the Chaplain has to say, Claire, before we jump to any conclusions, okay?"

"Right, we can't just jump to conclusions. I know that." Claire turned back toward the men and peppered them with more questions. "How bad is it? Did you say there was a bomb? How close was she to the explosion? Was it one of those IUD's? No, wait, that's birth control."

"You mean an IED, an improvised explosive device? Yes, ma'am, we think it was."

"Oh God." Claire folded against Jordan. "Oh God, Jordie, it's bad."

"We'll work it out. Please, let's hear what else the Chaplain has to say, honey, before we—"

"I know, I know, before we jump to conclusions."

"I'm sorry, Father, please continue." Claire could barely look at the man.

"She's been stabilized and is being flown out to Germany. She took a pretty bad hit. I don't have all the details of her injuries, but I understand that one of those with her died at the scene."

"Oh God," Claire whispered. Nic survived and one of her men was killed, just like before. Nic would be devastated. "Oh Nic," Claire groaned, tears falling again as she thought about the turmoil Nic had gone through before, being the only survivor of her helicopter crash in Iraq. Her injuries had seemed minor to Nic considering the death of her crew. Her scars were a constant reminder of their sacrifice for country.

"Nic's strong, honey. She'll make it, she's a survivor." Jordan rubbed Claire's arms and shoulders, trying to comfort her.

"How bad is she hurt, Father?"

The Chaplain looked down at his hands and twisted his wedding ring around nervously. Looking down at her own hand, she touched her own wedding ring. Suddenly her body contorted with the pain, drawing her into a semi-fetal position as she sat on the couch. Anguish flooded her mind; she needed to go to Nic, be with her.

"I wish I had more news, Mrs. Monroe, but I don't—"

"I want to be with her, where is she?"

"Well," he said. His voice was laced with caution. Swallowing hard, he looked at the captain who was with him and then back at Claire. They weren't telling her something. "As I said earlier, she's on a transport to Germany and then I suspect they'll send her to Walter Reed in D.C."

"When?"

"I don't have that information, yet. I'll call command in Germany and see if we can get an ETA for her departure from there."

"I want to talk to her, I want to hear her voice for myself and make sure she's okay. Where is she?"

Each man looked at the other and then back at Claire. "I'm not sure she's able to get a phone call at the moment, ma'am."

Something was wrong. There was something

they weren't telling her, she could feel it. The military was famous for not telling everything that happened in an accident. Hell, she'd lived through it, she knew from experience.

"What aren't you telling me?" Claire spiked for a moment, defiant in her command.

"Ma'am, I've told you all I can tell you. I'm sorry, as I said, she'll be transported to Walter Reed when she's stabilized," the priest said.

Claire looked at Jordan, her lips quivering as she tried to talk. "I want to be there when she arrives, at Walter Reed," Claire said, motioning with her hands. "I don't want her to be alone."

"We'll get you there, kiddo. Don't worry." Jordan tried to sound reassuring, but she wasn't pulling it off.

"Well, Mrs. Monroe. I'm sure the captain will be in contact with any further information."

The captain reached into a pocket, extracted a card, and handed it to her. He hadn't said much during the notification, so the sound of his deep voice shook Claire a little. "My number is on there as well as my email address. Please let me know if you need any assistance and I'll see what I can do to find out the status of Lt. Colonel Caldwell's injuries."

"Thank you," Jordan said, taking the card.

"Thanks." It was all Claire could eke out as she leaned on Jordan. She didn't think she could stand to see them out; her body was having a visceral reaction to the news of Nic being injured.

"You can see yourselves out, right?" Jordan said, pulling Claire's head onto her lap.

"Of course," the men said, a small smile offered in condolence.

Claire heard them whisper between them. "God,

I'm glad I don't have to do these often, Father."

"Strength, my son. They need you to be strong," the priest said, patting the captain on the shoulder reassuringly. "Strength."

"Why don't we get you into bed and you can take a nap," Jordan offered.

"I'm not tired, Jordan."

"I know, but maybe a little rest and…"

"What…you think that everything will be fine when I wake up? That it'll be a bad dream?" Claire said; the bite in her words couldn't be missed.

"Of course not, Claire."

"I'm sorry, Jordan. I just…I mean I just can't believe this is happening again."

"It isn't happening again. Nic's alive, injured, but she's alive. So just hold on to that."

"I need to be with her. I want her to know that I'm here and…" Claire looked down at her shaking hands and started to cry again. "That I love her. I can't lose her, Jordie. I just found her and I can't lose her."

"You're not going to lose her, kitten." Jordan ran her fingers through Claire's hair. "She knows you love her so don't worry. It'll all work out. Nic is strong, she's survived worse than this."

"How do we know this isn't worse? How do we know she isn't lying there on the verge of death? She could be taking her last breath as we speak and I'm not there to hold her hand, to be there with her. To comfort her and tell her how wonderful my life has been with her in it." Claire jumped off the couch and started pacing, anxiety replaced anguish, and fear amplified her pain. "I need to be with her, Jordie. I need to find out where she is and I need to be there."

Jordan grabbed her shoulders and tried to stop

her from pacing; she only succeeded in as far as Claire was rocking back and forth in place now. Claire's gaze darted around the room as she tried to focus on what she needed to do to get to Nic.

Passports for her and Grace, airline tickets, cash, clothes. Oh God, let her be okay. Please, please let her be okay, she pleaded internally.

"Claire." Jordan shook her a little rougher this time. "Claire, we don't know when she's getting shipped back to the states, so we should just wait for word. The captain said he would call when he found out any information."

"Something's wrong, Jordan. I can feel it. Did you see the way they avoided me when I said I wanted to talk to her? Stabilize, what does that mean?"

"Honey, let's not jump to conclusions, okay? I'm sure they have a strict protocol they have to follow. With HIPA and all those new laws, they probably can't just tell you."

"Bullshit." Claire jerked away from Jordan. "They knew more than they were saying, I know it."

Claire charged to her bedroom, tossed a suitcase on the bed, and started stuffing it with clothes, not paying attention to what she was throwing in the case more than trying to take back some control over the life events that were spiraling out of control.

Claire shuffled through the closet, searching for stuff to take to Germany. That *was* where Nic was, right? She questioned herself. Everything had happened so fast, she couldn't pay attention beyond hearing the words, "There's been an accident." Pulling her jacket out, she accidently grabbed Nic's instead. Claire held it up to her nose; taking a deep breath, she could still smell Nic on it, her cologne, her scent. It all came rushing at Claire. Falling to her knees, she clung to the only thing that she felt linked her to Nic at that moment. Rubbing her cheek against it, she took a deep breath and inhaled her lover's scent over and over again.

Why, why, why?

It was all she could think of, why? Hadn't they paid their dues? How could God be so cruel and do this to Nic, again? Nic didn't deserve this. She would gladly trade places with Nic and told God as much. What God? If there was a God, then why did he let people suffer, why did he take every happiness she and Nic shared and seemingly toss it all away for them? No, for Claire there wasn't a just God, there was just God. She started weeping so hard she couldn't control herself. Her body wracked with pain, still clutching Nic's jacket to her chest.

"Stop," Jordan said, grabbing Claire's hands. "Just stop. If Grace sees you like this, you'll freak her out."

Claire froze. Grace. What would she say to Grace? Their lives had been tossed upside down once before and they'd survived, but they'd survived because of Nic. Nic had been their anchor in the storm, only now the waves were bigger and crashing again. Jordan helped her up and sat her on the bed.

"Maybe you should rest, kitten. This isn't how you want Grace to see you, is it?"

Claire shook her head, rolled to her side, and wrapped Nic's jacket around her, imaging it was Nic's arms around her. If she tried hard enough, she could almost make herself believe everything was going to be all right. Closing her eyes, she heard Jordan say something to Grace as she shut the bedroom door.

What would she tell Grace?

Chapter Eighteen

Nic heard noise around her and, turning towards it, she tried to force her eyes open but something stopped them from complying. Reaching up, she felt her face. Gauze covered her eyes. Nic tried to speak but her mouth wouldn't move.

What the hell is going on, she thought. The harder she tried to talk, the more painful it became. She was in a world of darkness and she couldn't see, she couldn't speak, and she had no idea where she was or how to get help. She slipped a finger inside her lip and felt the wires keeping her mouth shut. The pain shooting through her face was excruciating. The more she tried to work her mouth open, the worse it got. Finally, she groaned when a sharp pain shot through her jaw.

"Colonel, you're okay. You're just waking up from some medication we had to give you to keep you still. I was just getting ready to remove the bandages before you woke up. Try and relax."

Nic felt the cold steel of scissors slide between the side of her face and the gauze. The sound as they sliced through the material sent a quick shiver, giving her goose bumps. Dim light started to peek through as someone pulled the bandages away from her face. She'd barely opened them when another sharp pain radiated in her head. The lights in the room weren't on, but it was bright enough that Nic shielded her eye.

Her right eye remained covered.

"Don't open your eye too quickly. Let it get acclimated to the light in the room," someone said, but Nic still couldn't see them.

Nic tried to force her eye open, but it felt so heavy, like weights were keeping it closed, and again it fell closed. A beeping sound caught her attention, so she focused on that. It sounded like...a heartbeat, *her heartbeat?* Pushing herself, she just needed to sit up, get her feet under her, and she would be fine, she kept telling herself. Forcing herself up, she tried to reach for something, anything to assist her in a futile attempt to stand. At least she thought she could stand.

"Colonel, you need to lie still," said someone she didn't recognize.

Nic could only hear a garbled noise as she tried to answer.

"Colonel, your jaw is wired shut. Would you like a sip of water?"

Confused, Nic could only see shadows when a light from a pen light snapped on somewhere in the room. She opened her mouth and tried to say something again, but the pain almost made her black out. Her head reeled and hit the pillow before she could do anything. The headache was unbearable and she could use something for the pain.

Christ, what the fuck happened, she thought. Her mind was blank as she tried to remember where she was and what had happened.

She flinched as someone touched her arm.

"It's all right, Colonel. I just need to listen to your lungs and I'll call the doctor in so he can brief you on what's happened." A stethoscope touched her chest, followed by an order to take a deep breath.

Cough, cough. She couldn't take a deep breath. *What the hell was wrong with her?*

"That's okay, Colonel. After what you've been through, I'm surprised you're awake."

Nic focused in on the woman's voice, trying to see her, but she could only make out the blue of her scrubs out of her left eye. The blood pressure cuff squeezed around her bicep and then released.

"Your blood pressure is a little low, so no getting out of bed without help. Okay?"

Nic gave a brief nod and then closed her eyes. The strain of the light was making her headache worse.

"Would you like a sip of water?"

Nodding, she tried opening her mouth just as the pain gave her a sharp reminder that she couldn't. A groan was the only thing slipping past her lips at the moment.

"I'm going to raise your head a little, so you can take a sip."

A straw was placed against Nic's lips. Grabbing the tip between her lips, she took a long, slow pull. Water never tasted so good, so…she choked as it hit the back of her dry throat.

"Slowly, Colonel. If you get sick, you'll suffocate in your own vomit."

Now that's a gross predicament, Nic thought, releasing the straw as it was pulled away.

"Let me get the doctor, Colonel." With that, the lights went off again. The darkness was soothing in an odd sort of way and Nic's world faded to black. The pain ate at the edges of her consciousness so she couldn't go back to sleep. Her body ached all over and if she had to say what happened, her best guess was she'd been hit by a bus.

"Good evening, Colonel Caldwell. I hear you're awake."

A deep voice echoed in her head and the bright lights added and amplified the pain she was in. She wanted to grab her head but she could barely lift her left hand. *Christ!*

That's debatable, Nic thought, trying to focus on the doctor. The fluorescent lights behind him made it hard for Nic to see his face. It didn't matter, he was blurry anyway.

"I'm sure you're in a lot of pain, Colonel. This is a morphine pump for the pain," he said, lifting the device up so she could see it better. "Since we can't give you anything by mouth, you can still get some relief by pushing this. However, you can push it all you want, but it will only dispense a set amount."

Nic nodded.

"So, how much do you remember, Colonel?"

Nic shook her head and tried to mouth the word nothing.

Patting her hand reassuringly, he said, "That's probably just as well. First, you're in Germany and as soon as I think you're ready to travel, we're going to send you back to the states to Walter Reed. They are set up to help you as you recover. You also need some reconstructive surgery."

Nic's brow furrowed as she grunted, "Why?"

"Are you having trouble focusing?"

She nodded.

"Your orbital socket is blown out and your cheek is broken. We think a bone is pinching the orbital nerve and we need to get in there and fix it before it becomes permanent and you go blind in that eye. You have a broken arm, most of the bones in your hand were crushed, you have three broken ribs, a broken jaw, and shrapnel in your face and neck. Your left femur has a series of hairline fractures, but those should heal relatively quickly."

Nic tried to tick off the laundry list of broken bones and injuries but she couldn't focus on everything being said as he quickly rattled it off. She made a writing motion with her hand.

"Would you like a pen and paper?"

Nic pointed to him and whispered, "You…write."

"Oh, you want me to write it all down?" He took a pad and pen from his white lab coat and started scribbling, walking to her right. "I don't want you to worry, Co…."

Out of her peripheral, she could see his lips moving, so she turned towards him and picked up the last few things he said.

"…I think the fact that you're young and strong will aid in your recovery. It should go well."

Nic cleared her throat, trying to get his attention.

"Oh, I'm sorry." He looked up.

Nic slowly raised her left hand, tapped her right ear, and shook her head. "Can't…ear"

"You can't hear out of your right ear?"

Nic shook her head again; the pain spiked with each twist.

The doctor's smile dimmed momentarily and then slipped back into place. He walked back over to the left side and pulled a chair around, facing her. "I'd like to try and start to get you sitting up and doing breathing treatments. I don't want pneumonia to set in, Colonel. Also, if you can bear it I'd like to try and get you out of bed. I'm checking the surgery rotation to see when I can get you in a fix that orbital fracture and your cheek bone."

"Wife…I…"

"Ah, your wife. I haven't had time to contact her. I understand that the Marine Corps has sent someone to let her know that you've been wounded, but—"

"NO," Nic said, trying to right herself in the bed. She didn't want Claire to worry, but it was already too late. "When?"

"When did they contact her?" The doctor looked down at Nic's chart and then at his watch. "You've been out for about three days, Colonel. We had to sedate you and put you in a semi-comatose state due to some swelling around the brain. The explosion was—"

"Stop." Nic put her left hand up. "Stop, peese," she barely hissed out.

Her mind raced. Claire, explosion, what the hell happened and how was she going to talk to Claire? The last time someone came to the house, it was her telling Claire that Mike was dead. Now Claire had another visit from the Marine Corps and she could only imagine how frantic Claire was right now. Nic touched her lips, her hand making a drinking motion.

"Aw, thirsty. Nurse, can we have some water for the Colonel?" He looked back at Nic, who was now making a writing motion. "Of course, here, I'll hold it for you." He handed Nic the pen, flipped the page, and rested the pad against the hospital bed rail.

Nic scrawled across as best she could across the pad, but it was barely legible. Children learning to write had better handwriting than she did at the moment. Pulling the pen back, she pointed to the pad. *Who knew writing could be so taxing,* she thought as she dropped her hand to the bed.

No wife.

"You don't want me to call your wife, Colonel?"

Nic nodded her head and then shook it. She wanted him to call her and tell her everything was fine and not to worry, but Nic also wanted him to tell Claire to stay home. She didn't want Claire to see, not like this.

Nic motioned to write again. Scribbling something on the pad, she turned it towards him.

"Home, you can't go home yet, Colonel. I'm sorry, we need to stabilize you before we can risk another transport."

Nic shook her head and pointed to the word *wife* and then *home*.

"You want your wife to stay home. You don't want her to come here," he said, pointing to the floor.

Nic nodded, the pain spiking each time she did.

"I'll see what I can do, Colonel. I doubt she'll come all the way to Germany if she knows we're going to be sending you to Walter Reed." He offered a slight smile.

He didn't know Claire Monroe.

Nic motioned for the pad again and scribbled something else.

The doctor turned the pad and stared at it for a moment. "It's a good thing I can read doctor writing, I think this is asking me what happened to you. Right?"

Nic nodded briefly and tried to take a deep breath, but her chest felt constricted and she could only manage a shallow pull. A quick sip and the water was taken away again. How was she ever going to be able to get out of bed if she couldn't drink, let alone eat something? Her mind wandered as the push of morphine from earlier started to eat away at the pain and her mind.

She jutted her chin towards the pad and looked up at the doctor.

"Colonel Caldwell, do you remember anything before today?"

Nic shook her head.

"Do you remember being stationed in Afghanistan?"

Nic's brows furrowed. She searched the bed as if it would give up her secrets, but it wasn't any use. She couldn't remember much—Josh, the corporal at Camp Leatherneck. She remembered him. A civilian, she remembered working with a civilian…Max something…and an Army sergeant doing something… what were they doing…driving in the desert.

Nic stretched as she tried to untwist herself in the backseat of the Humvee. No matter how hard she worked the muscles in her neck, the crick in it was starting to feel like it was a permanent part of her body. She wrapped the wool blanket around herself and tried to look out of the narrow windows. The morning cold had fogged them and the sun hadn't hit them to warm them up yet. Reaching for her water, she flinched when she picked up a half frozen water bottle. She'd have to put it on the hood when they started the Humvee if she wanted to drink it today. It had been her turn to sleep in the back seat. Sergeant Ramirez was behind her in the smaller compartment. Lucky for everyone she was the tinier of the three and fit. Otherwise, the crick in Nic's neck would be a full body one, from her neck to her knees.

Taking out a zip lock bag, she unfolded a few baby wipes and tried her best to clean up. It would be a few days before they were back at base and a shower.

Thank God for baby wipes! All of her toiletries fit into a few zip lock bags and didn't take up much room in her ruck. While men could go days without a shower, she, on the other hand, could not. Basic hygiene was essential to her mental state. She didn't care if the rest of the crew stunk, but she wasn't going to. Pulling out her toothbrush, she squirted a dab of toothpaste and grabbed the water bottle. There was enough to brush and rinse if she was miserly with it. Tossing her brush in her mouth, she waited a minute, as she stretched her arms across the top of the seats and listened to the quiet.

Tea, what she wouldn't do for a hot cup of Darjeeling tea, with cream and sugar.

"Colonel?"

Nic searched the doctor's face, desperate for answers.

"Do you remember what happened?"

She squeezed her eyes shut and gave a short nod. Making a writing motion again, she grasped the pen and scribbled some more. Twisting the pad towards the doctor, he mouthed what she'd written.

"Who died?" The doctor gave her a confused look. "Colonel, you need to focus on your recovery and not—"

Nic jabbed her finger at the paper insistently. She needed to know.

"Who," she grunted. "Who."

She'd get an assessment of her injuries later, but this was important. She was alive again and she wanted to know who'd sacrificed their lives just to get some tribal information for the government.

The doctor pulled the curtain around them as if it would keep out the world, or prevent the rest of the bay from hearing what he had to say.

The full-bird colonel sat back in the chair and took a deep breath. If Nic didn't know better, she was about to be counseled. The only thing missing was a counseling slip that usually accompanied these sessions.

"Your team was in the accident. A civilian, Max Drummond, and an Army sergeant Cecilia Ramirez. The sergeant came back with you on the medical transport." Nic visibly sighed; her lips let the breath push through. "The civilian, however, wasn't as lucky. I'm afraid he died of his injuries. I'm sorry, Colonel. This damn deployment has cost us dearly and we signed up for this, but a civilian, well....." He didn't say anything for a moment. "Anything else?"

Nic nodded and made the writing sign again. Her throat was too dry to talk and her jaw was killing her from trying to move against the wires.

Flipping the page back, she pointed to what she had written before.

"Ah, you want to know what happened and what your injuries are, okay." He scrubbed the stubble on his chin, clenched his jaw, and stretched out his neck. "From what I understand from the report, you were hit by an IED. If you had been inside the armored Humvee, you and your team would have probably been fine. It seems that you all had just exited the vehicle and one of your team detonated it by stepping on it. Probably Mr. Drummond since he was killed."

The click, Nic remembered. The scene flashed back right in front of her. Damn.

Nic motioned her finger around her body and cast a questioning look at the doctor.

"Your injuries, well, you must have been pretty

close to Mr. Drummond. I have a copy of the report right here. I'm going to leave it for you to read, when you're ready. This isn't normal protocol but unfortunately I'm late for my rounds," he said, looking down at his watch. "We're going to get you into surgery to fix that crushed orbital socket and your broken cheek. So get some rest."

Chapter Nineteen

The smell of antiseptic took Claire back to the last time she was in a hospital, Grace's birth. The cold sterile environment, the muted chatter drifting from the rooms to mingle in the halls, the scurry of nurses dressed in the same type of scrubs, and doctors wearing dress greens under their lab coats were all reminders she wasn't in a civilian world. Claire had been told to report to the fourth floor nurses' station and she suspected this was where Nic was. Her instructions at the front desk of the hospital had been clear and precise, report to the fourth floor nurses' station and be prepared to wait.

"Can I help you?" A nurse said dispassionately, barely looking up from what Claire assumed was a set of charts. The nurses' station was an exercise in controlled chaos. When one nurse moved out of the hive, another took her place, clearing charts, writing orders, or giving orders to someone.

"Yes, I'm here to see Colonel Caldwell," she said to the hive buzzing in unison.

"Only immediate family is allowed to see the Colonel," said no one in particular. The Hive mentality was working well, as expected.

Claire had remembered to grab their marriage license, and power of attorney. She left anticipating that the moment she said wife, proof would be required. She'd barely remembered to have Nic sign the sponsorship paperwork so she could get a new dependent ID card. She pinched the bridge of her nose. The things that the military made families do that civilians had no concept about.

Pulling her dependent ID, her power of attorney, and her marriage license, she held it over the counter and said, "Will this do?"

"Ma'am?" One of the nurses said. She had the look and the rank of a charge nurse, so Claire gave a brief smile and handed her the documents.

"Dependent ID, marriage license, and power of attorney," she said, looking down at the documents the nurse still hadn't looked at yet. "I've flown for the last fourteen hours, had three layovers, and left a daughter half way around the world, so I'd like to see my wife. Please."

She hadn't meant to sound like one of *those wives or mothers*, but she needed to see Nic with her own eyes and put her worst fears to rest.

"I'll get the doctor who's treating Colonel Caldwell, Mrs. Caldwell."

She wanted to correct the nurse and explain she wasn't Mrs. Caldwell, but at the moment it would only confuse everyone and put her under more scrutiny, so screw it. She and Nic hadn't talked about changing names; there wasn't time. They'd married so quickly, but now Claire wished she was Mrs. Caldwell; at least she was in her heart.

"Please follow me," a slender woman said, motioning for Claire. There wasn't any small talk between them, they hadn't exchanged niceties, the nurse moved like a buzz saw through the people milling about in the halls. Opening a door, she instructed Claire to wait inside the office. The nametag said Dr.

Morton. The small office was crammed with stuff and only a few pictures sat on the only sparsely populated bookshelf. Across from it was a wall with a diploma prominently displayed its importance amongst the other clutter of a doctor's office clearly defined.

"I'll let the doctor know you're here. I don't think he was expecting you," she said, stating the obvious.

"Thank you," Claire said curtly, again the stress of the travel and fear of what she would find coloring her voice. She turned her back on the nurse, and took the only clear seat across from the desk. She studied the diploma again.

Stanford.

Impressive. Now she had to wonder what made a person with a Stanford degree want to practice medicine in the military. Not that it wasn't a good career choice, but Stanford came with a certain prestige. So what made a man who could open any door with a degree from Stanford want to be an Army doctor? The assignment to a field hospital, the long hours, and lost family time didn't make for great career opportunities, but that was just her opinion. A few other certificates dotted the wall. They were all Greek to her, but as long as he was a good doctor, she didn't care if he wore a tutu after work. It was what he did at work that mattered to Claire.

She texted Jordan, letting her know she'd made it to Germany. She already missed Grace, but the long trip and the last minute accommodations had made the decision easy. Grace would stay home with Jordan.

"We are doing great. Getting ready to put Grace down for the night." Jordan texted. "Hitting the pool tomorrow."

"Don't pick up any strays." Claire texted back,

smiling at the inference.

"Aw, you're no fun. Give Nic a kiss and tell her we love her. See you soon."

"Thanks, I'll call when I get back to the room."

"K."

Tucking the phone back in her purse, she shifted in the chair. The office was stifling, so Claire opened the door, turned the chair a little to the side so she could enjoy the slight breeze in the hallway. People of various uniforms passed the door. Doctors and nurses going over charts, interns pushing patients in wheelchairs and beds passed. None took notice of Claire, who nervously bounced her knee up and down. She wasn't sure she could wait much longer. Searching the hall for anyone who might stop her progress, she grabbed her purse and decided to find Nic's room herself.

Walking down the halls, she peered into rooms and tried look without really looking. If she didn't spot a familiar face, she casually moved down the hall to the next door. As she hit one door, a nurse came and they almost collided.

"Oh, I'm sorry. Can I help you?" the nurse said, tucking a chart under her arm and disposing of rubber gloves in the trash by the door.

"Oh gosh, I hope so. I think I'm lost. I went to the bathroom and now I can't find my spouse's room. Perhaps you can help me get reoriented?" Claire smiled and turned in a circle looking around the hallway for emphasis.

"Of course. Who's your husband?"

Without missing a beat, Claire said, "Colonel Nic Caldwell."

A momentary look of shock crossed the woman's

face, but she recovered quickly. "I see, well, I think the Colonel is one hallway over. Come with me and I'll take you there."

"I can't thank you enough. This place is so—"

"Busy?"

"Gosh, I had no idea it was so big and well, you're doing an amazing job here. I can't imagine what it's like to get the wounded from Afghanistan. I guess you've seen everything here?"

"Pretty much. I've definitely earned my bars at this place. My first stop after nursing school and it's pretty much an adrenaline rush, depending on the floor you work. I was in emergency first and now I'm on the floor with the patients. I like it a lot better. You get to know them and well..."

"I understand," Claire said, putting her hand on the nurse's arm. "It can be overwhelming."

"Are you a nurse?"

"Oh no, I've just sorta gone through this before. My first husband was killed in Iraq."

"Oh wow, I'm so sorry." The nurse stopped and pointed to an open door. "This is Colonel Caldwell's room. Let me know if you need anything."

"Thank you," Claire said, searching her scrubs for a nametag. "Captain?"

"Smith."

"Captain Smith, thank you for your help."

"Of course. Good afternoon."

With that, she was down the hall and gone. Claire thought she'd prepared herself for how Nic might look, even the possibility of missing an arm or a leg, but the actuality of coming face-to-face with Nic was beyond anything she could have imagined. Her stomach clenched and tried to give up its meager breakfast of coffee and a stale donut, the best they had at the USO room at the stateside airport. Claire's own body contracted at the way Nic's body contorted in pain. Claire turned back into the hallway. She clasped her hand to her throat, trying to swallow the lump that threatened to choke her. She leaned against the cold cement wall, resting her head back against it. She sucked in a lungful of air and forced it out through pursed lips. Her head started to spin and her world felt like it would topple out of orbit. She couldn't stop the tears that trailed down her face. Her lover lay broken and battered in a hospital half way around the world and all Claire wanted to do was scoop her up and take her home, to their home, and make the world go way, forever.

Anger replaced pain as a thought hit her. She'd entrusted her lover's life to the military and they had returned her barely clinging to life, and now she had to wonder what kind of life lay ahead for Nic. A life of more pain; hadn't she paid enough when she was injured in Iraq? What more could the military ask of Nic? She burned inside thinking about everything they had gone through in the past four years. Mike's death, Nic's injuries in Iraq, and now, Nic lay in a bed surviving God knows what in Afghanistan.

Peeking around the corner, the only thing she could be thankful for right now other than the fact that Nic was asleep and hadn't seen her cringe was that Nic was alive. Claire would take that small gift for now. Trying to control the combination of emotions battling within her, she slipped on a mask of control and told herself she would weep later for her lover. Nic needed to see a strong supportive Claire, not one who needed Nic to be strong. It was Nic's turn to lean on Claire.

Claire could only make a cursory study of Nic. She was sleeping more upright than down. Her arm was in a sling, her wrist in a cast, and the whole limb was wrapped to her body. She couldn't see much more than that, but the blue and black bruising around Nic's eyes seeped all the way down into her cheeks. It rocked Claire to her core to see Nic so battered. Her heart shattered into tiny little pieces, with each piece slicing into her soul, knowing there was nothing she could do to stop the pain Nic was enduring. Little gouges that had scabbed over littered Nic's face. Even her strong lips were swollen and bruised. She wanted to touch Nic. To smooth her hair away from her face, to let her fingertips trail across the set lips, to let Nic know she was safe. But she didn't dare; Nic was a light sleeper and judging by her injuries, sleep was probably the best thing for her right now.

Her mothering instinct were taking over and like a bear guarding her cub, Claire looked around the room, dimming the lights, closing the door, and gently pulling up a thin blanket to cover Nic's body.

Claire sat back down and stared at Nic, tears breaking past her defenses and releasing themselves, creating a watery path down her face. Rifling through her purse, she looked for tissue. The best she could do was a wadded up cartoon one she had tossed in her purse earlier in the week.

Grace.

What would she tell Grace? Nothing. She had nothing to tell Grace, except Nic was alive and she would take that, for now. Claire crossed her arms and leaned her head against the wall. She willed her mind to go blank, but the only thing she could focus on was

Nic. She wished it was her in the bed, rather than Nic, but it wasn't to be. Please let her be okay, she prayed over and over again.

༄ ༄ ༄ ༄

The smell of something familiar drifted in the breeze, but Nic couldn't quite place it. The faster she walked, the more intense the smell became.
Perfume.
She ran in the darkness, but stumbled to her knees. Resting back on her heels, she looked around but there wasn't anything in front of her; behind her, there was nothing as far as the eye could see, but a hazy fog seemed to be moving towards her slowly. She felt a chill slice through her. Her body rebelled against the cold. Every muscle screamed at her to stop moving.

There it was again, that smell – only stronger this time. She could barely think right now, but something about it was familiar. Her mind latched on to it and wrestled until she finally realized it was Claire's perfume. The recognition made Nic smile; at least she could still focus on something. She tried to stand, but she couldn't get her legs under. So she low-crawled on her elbows. She had to keep moving forward. Where, she didn't know, she just knew if she stopped, she'd probably die in this God-forsaken hellhole. A pinprick of light pierced the haze, so she moved in that direction. The smell of Claire's perfume gave her a shot of adrenaline, propelling her towards the light. Thank God Claire wasn't here to see her like this. Nic knew she was a shell of the person who stood beside Claire when they recited their vows just a few months ago. She couldn't bear to look into Claire's eyes and know she would see pity. The pain of her broken body was something she could handle, but not Claire's pain.

Nic couldn't move any further, the pain had won. Groaning, she turned her head. She noticed light peeking through the drawn privacy curtain and Claire sleeping across from her. The side effects from the pain medication were brutal. Now she was hallucinating. Claire sleeping across from her almost felt real, so real if she could she would reach out and touch her, but she didn't. On the one hand, she couldn't live with the disappointment, and on the other, a dream was almost as good as the real thing for Nic.

Resting her head back against the bed, she closed her eyes and willed herself to dream of Claire, of that day in the backyard, just before she'd told Claire she was being shipped to Afghanistan. It had been the last time they were intimate and Nic had played that day over and over again in her head so many times, she could smell Claire, just as she could now.

At least in her dreams, she was the strong protector and lover she always saw herself to be. At least she had her dreams.

Chapter Twenty

Claire jumped as a hand tapped her shoulder. She'd fallen asleep. Making sure Nic was still asleep, she looked up and found a man in a lab coat over dress greens pressing a finger to his lips and motioning to the hallway.

She'd been found out. Panic surged through her as she looked down the hallway. Feeling like a kid, she wanted to run; knowing she was an adult, she stood her ground.

"Mrs. Caldwell?" he said in a hushed tone.

"Yes." She hesitated correcting him, so she let it slide.

His consternation was conveyed through a steely set of gunmetal gray eyes. How appropriate, Claire thought. She wouldn't be intimidated though. She straightened up, squared her body directly as him, and waited. She noticed he held a wrapped package under his arm.

"I'm Doctor Morton," he said, extending his hand. The soft handshake threw her off. Clearly, he wasn't here to admonish her, at least not yet, not in the hallway within earshot of Nic. "This is for you. There were instructions in her duffle bag that if something happened to her, you should have these."

"Claire." She offered her own name and then looked down at the large, non-descript, manila envelope. Squeezing it, she tried to make out what was inside. Opening it in front of the doctor would be inappropriate, so she'd wait until she was alone. "Dr. Morton. How's my wife doing?"

His lips set in a firm line before he spoke. "Let's get some coffee, Mrs. Caldwell."

The slow walk to the cafeteria allowed Claire to study the doctor as he interacted with the staff at the hospital. His gently manner was disguised by the ramrod look of authority he generated when someone wearing a uniform crossed his path. Short, succinct answers and directions that were clearly to be followed were given to a few that pitched their charts at him. He motioned her through the doors of the cafeteria and towards the coffee machine.

"Starbucks this isn't, but it will have to do." He smiled and handed her an empty cup.

"Good thing I drink tea then. You can't really screw that up." Claire poured hot water and grabbed a tea bag as she started to make her way to the cashier.

"No charge," the cashier said. "Afternoon Colonel. How's the wife and daughter?"

"Good, Marie, thanks for asking."

He guided them to a seat away from the tangle of trays and food being served, pulling out a seat for Claire.

"Thank you." She waited until he sat before she asked again. "So how is my wife, Dr. Morton?"

"Honestly? She's lucky to be alive," he said, blowing then sipping from his cup. "We just brought her out of a mini coma. We were worried about some swelling on the brain. It could have been from the transport, but most likely it was from her injuries."

Claire felt like she wanted to cry, but bit the inside of her lip, letting the pain momentarily distract her. "Does she have brain damage?" Her worst fears didn't even come close to encompassing brain damage. How could she have not thought of that? Oh God!

"Not that we can see. Her scans look good, but…" He sipped his coffee again.

"But what?"

He looked like he'd been up for hours already and rubbed at the day's growth on his chin then cleared his throat. "Her injuries aren't life threatening, but they are severe. She might be deaf in her right ear. We're going to have to take her into surgery to reconstruct her orbital socket that's blown out, she has a malar fracture–"

"What's that?" Claire interrupted.

"Oh, sorry. It's a broken cheekbone on her right side. The orbital facture is pinching her optic nerve so we need to get in there and take care of that; otherwise she could lose her sight in that eye."

"Oh God!" Claire's lip quivered and finally the tears started to fall again.

He reached over and patted her hand. "She'll go into surgery in the morning, so let's not worry quite yet. We are going to have a small problem with surgery though. She has a broken mandible."

Claire looked at him as if he was speaking Greek and shrugged her shoulders.

"Broken jaw. It's wired shut so we are going to have to make some adjustments when we intubate her."

"Oh God." Was all Claire could say, remembering how bad Nic looked earlier.

"She gonna be in some pain for a while. I won't lie to you, this is going to suck for her. She got three broken ribs, her right hand was crushed, her arm is broken, and she has a hairline fracture on her left femur. For the most part, all of her injuries are on her right side. If you think she looks bad now, she's going to look a little worse. We'll do our best to make her comfortable and keep the pain to a minimum, but honestly, she's going to be in a lot of pain. Her recovery is going to depend on how she manages her pain."

Claire felt sick again. She'd gone through childbirth and thought that pain was unbearable, but what the doctor was describing was way beyond anything she'd experienced and she wasn't sure she could handle seeing Nic in that kind of pain. She felt herself getting light-headed; a cold sweat broke across her face.

"Are you okay?" The doctor reached across the table and felt Claire's skin with the back of his hand.

"I'll be okay." Claire gave a half-hearted smile, waving his hand off.

"I'll get you some water. Do you feel like you're going to faint?"

"I'll be okay, I'm just a little tired."

"Here." He handed her a bottle of cold water. "Sip, slowly."

"What happened to Nic?" Claire asked, trying to take her mind off fainting. It happened anytime she was in a hospital; she was used to it. It would pass.

"IED, went off on her right side."

"Was anyone else hurt?"

"Civilian she was working with was killed and her gunner was injured as well, but not as bad. She's lucky to be alive, Mrs. Caldwell." He stared at her and then looked down at his coffee, running the wooden stick through the dark liquid. He'd probably given this type of talk to more than a few families, considering the amount of casualties and injuries in Afghanistan, lately. He didn't offer any over inflated hope, he didn't tell her to look at the bright side. He was as matter-of-fact as they came. His job wasn't to blow smoke up someone's ass, his was to fix the injured and move on to the next patient. She could just tell somehow that he'd done this a hundred times before.

Claire was on overload with all the information. She didn't know what to ask, so she just started firing questions at him.

"What's her prognosis? Will she be able to walk, to talk, to play with her daughter? When can she go home? What kind of life will she have after this?"

He bit his lip and grabbed her hands, folding them together. "Mrs. Caldwell...slow down...I know I've given you a lot of bad news, but I want you to try and think about Colonel Caldwell for a moment. Let's just focus on getting her through surgery in the morning and then we can tackle the other things. We want to fix that optical nerve so she doesn't lose her vision. Everything else will just take time. Okay?"

She nodded her head. He was right, they needed to take care of the most severe things first, but she wanted Nic back now.

"There is something else you should know," he said. "She didn't want you here."

"What?"

"I'm sorry, I'm sure that's difficult for you to hear, but it isn't uncommon for a soldier to wait to see their family. As you can see, she's pretty beat up and she looks like death warmed over. Would you want someone to see you like that?"

"She's a proud woman, but I'm her wife and this

is where I should be," Claire said, trying to reassure herself as much as the doctor.

"Well, don't be surprised if she isn't happy to see you tomorrow. As you said, she's a proud Marine and proud Marines don't like to be seen as weak, and right now she couldn't be any more dependent on someone than she will be for the next several months. So be prepared, it may not go as you think."

Claire hadn't thought that Nic wouldn't want her around. The thought never crossed her mind. Her place was with Nic, fighting just as hard as Nic would for her. But what if...she stopped herself, she would just have to deal with it when it happened. No use asking for trouble if it didn't exist. Right?

Chapter Twenty-one

Nic couldn't swallow, the light was piercing, and she couldn't feel the right side of her face. She ran her fingertips across her lip; she couldn't feel it. A beeping rang in her ears and she felt like she'd been the guest of honor at a blanket party. Reaching for her mouth, she felt her jaw wired shut again. She let out a groan that got someone's attention. When she didn't hear anyone, she tried to sit up.

"Hey, hey, hold on there, Colonel."

A nurse stepped into her field of vision, but she could only see out of one eye. Tapping the tube, she grunted.

"Okay, hold on. We wired your jaw shut after surgery, you're probably pretty sore. Your blood pressure was so low we almost lost you in there, Colonel. You're just coming out of surgery, so try and relax. If you can't, I'll give you something to make you less combative. Do you understand?" She smiled and patted Nic's exposed shoulder.

Nic lay back on the bed and pulled the sheet, trying to cover herself.

"Here, this is a warm blanket. It'll keep you warm until we get you back to your room."

An IV was still stuck into her wrist, heart monitor pads pulled on her chest as she tried to adjust her blanket. Picking up the blanket and sheet, she realized she was naked.

Great, she thought. All she wanted was to get back to her room, and be left alone. Running her hand over her face, she felt bandages covering the right side of her face.

"Colonel, I understand you're awake." Dr. Morton appeared into her field of view. "You're gonna feel like a train wreck when the medication wears off, but we've still got you on a morphine drip. Same situation, press it when you're feeling crappy. I think we were able to clear the optic nerve. We've reconstructed your orbital socket and cheek. I can't vouch for how pretty you're gonna look when all the swelling goes down, but you'll be able to see."

Nic nodded her head, closed her eye, and drifted back asleep.

※ ※ ※ ※

Claire had barely gotten off a quick kiss on the forehead when they wheeled her off to surgery and now she waited for word. She clutched the manila envelope to her chest, as if doing so would comfort her. Claire stared at it and thought for a moment that she shouldn't open it. She should save it for Nic and let Nic decide if Claire should see its contents or not. Nic's instructions had been if anything happened to her, not if she died. Flipping it over, she tugged at the red string that wrapped around the grommets keeping it closed. Pulling it around, and then back and around again, Claire broke the seal and opened the envelope. Peering inside, she noticed a few photographs, folded paper, and the journal Claire had given Nic before she deployed.

Claire tipped the envelope, and the journal,

Nic's wedding ring, and photographs filled her hand. Blood splatters covered the journal and photos. Claire peeled the top photo from the stack; it crackled as the blood cracked and broke off. Smiling, she recognized it as the last one they'd taken at the Marine Corps Ball. Nic looked dashing in her uniform, small medals hanging from her chest. Her hands held Claire's and the smile, well, it was classic Nic Caldwell charming.

Her eyes clouded as she looked over at her wife, battered and beaten in the bed across from her. The Nic lying in the hospital bed might never be the same Nic in her hands. She couldn't stop the tears from falling and mixing with the dried blood on the journal, smearing them together across it as she tried to wipe them away.

Claire lovingly ran a finger across Nic's face on the photo, as if she could feel her soft lips. That night had been freeing in that they didn't have to hide who they were. They had attended as a couple, had their picture taken, and danced like every other couple that night. They had come a long way, but she wasn't taking anything for granted; she still felt like they still had a ways to go.

She tucked the photo back with the rest, slipped them back into the envelope, and stuffed it back into her purse. Wiping her tears away, she set the journal in her lap and stared at it. The edges were darker, signaling that the journal had been used. Blood dotted the leather, while the leather thong was still tied tight, securing its closure. Her fingers caressed the edges up and down and then rested on top of the cover. She closed her eyes and waited.

Was she ready to read what was inside? She instructed Nic to tell her what her days were like overseas. She'd practically ordered her to keep the journal, thinking it would be something they could share when Nic got home. A peek, so to speak, inside Nic's life in Afghanistan and yet she wasn't sure she wanted to know. Now she sat cradling the journal, ready to read Nic's thoughts, to see her words, to feel what she felt when she'd written them down. Knowing Nic, it would be uncensored, raw, and full of emotion. Nic unguarded.

Pulling on the knot, she laid each thong open and waited again. If she was having second thoughts, now was the time to stop. She reminded herself Nic had said she should have it if anything happened. Looking over at Nic, she waited as if Nic would tell her it was okay. Nic's slow shallow breathing gave Claire an easy peace.

Picking up the leather, she pushed the cover back. The paper cracked open and exposed another photographed tucked between the cover and the first page where Claire had written a dedication to Nic. Flipping the photograph over, Claire smiled again. They'd taken the picture together in their backyard when they'd been goofing off. Grace photo bombed them, her head and eyes barely in the picture at the bottom. It had been a great day as she remembered the BBQ. Lifting the photo to her nose, she closed her eyes. She could almost smell the smoke. Life had a way of being a cruel mistress if this was their new normal, she thought, tucking the photo back between the pages. She looked at the inscription, but didn't bother to read it.

Thumbing the first page, she tried to pull it back, but blood had glued several pages together like a wax seal that kept secrets closed from prying eyes.

Her stomach lurched as she thought about how much blood Nic had to lose to cover the journal. Bending the pages, she felt them flex before they broke apart. Fine dust covered the first pages Claire opened the journal to. A dirty light brown film covered the pen indentations on the page and nestled in the seam.

Claire couldn't help herself as she ran a finger over Nic's telltale signature at the bottom of the page. Moving along the script as if she were penning it herself, her eyes followed the words, mouthing each word individually, savoring each as she read Nic's first entry.

Day 1

My first entry. I'm not sure how I let you convince me this was a good idea, but you usually know best, so I'll play along, for now. I thought about putting dates down, but I know I'll forget the month, let alone the day, so I'll just write whatever is going on over here. So here we go—I'm on a flight packed with men and women in battle gear (that stuff that protects us). We picked up our weapons, ammo, and plates, as they call 'em. I know what you're asking—what are plates? The easiest way to explain them is they stop the bullet, like bulletproof vests, sorta. I hope I never have to find out if they work. I want you to know you're never far from me. I have you tucked right next to my heart, baby! Forever, Nic.

Day 1 ½

I know it's too soon to be writing, but the rush of landing into Leatherneck was like a roller coaster and it's an adrenaline junkie's fix. Our decent was steep to avoid fire from those just waiting to take down a military jet. Glad they raised that SGLI cause you'd need it if this bitch crashed. I'm pumped and you wanted to know what it's like to be here.

Love ya.

N

Day 3

I know I said I wasn't going to post days, but it's early and I'm fresh. I think I must be going to heaven 'cause hell is called Afghanistan. 115 today! Met my gunner, Sgt. Ramirez, she isn't much of a talker, which is fine if she's a good shot! Seems like a stand-up gal. Quiet in that angry sorta way. Claire, my love, you took my breath away just seeing you on chat. Close enough to touch and yet beyond my reach. It killed me to say goodbye and shut the computer down. Gonna have to talk to that civilian and give him the lay of the land, asshole. Forever your lover,

N

Day 6

Not writing as often as I'd hoped, sorry. Getting ready to do our first jaunt outside the walls. Met our interpreter, Ami. He is just a kid, nice but a kid. Fingers crossed it all goes well. Love you baby! Had a dream about you last night, it was sexy as hell.

N

Day 9

We're out and amongst the locals. They look at us suspiciously. Can't blame 'em. This place is desolate, often makes me thankful for where we live. The stars were beautiful tonight. I wonder if you look out at them and think of me.
Love you!
N

P.S. Found out why Ramirez is so angry. You should see her scars, Claire—they're bad. Whole back seared. She hates our civie Drummond. Says there is something up with him. My gut says she might be right. He's a prick.

Day 12

Handed out soccer balls for the kids and Drummond gave something to the locals. Not sure what it was since he met them with our translator, Ami. Ami is a nice kid. I've been snapping some pics with my phone, was told I shouldn't be doing it. Fuck Drummond. I'll send them later.
Love you,
N

Day 14

The heat sucks! It has a way of wearing you down...I'll write more when I get back to base. Just know I'm thinking of you and Grace.
N

Day 16

...sorry time is getting away from me over here. It's depressing being out in the field all the time. I'll write when I have some down time. God, I miss you baby!
N

Day 20

God, what I wouldn't give for a shower. Baby wipes in a zipper bag is our version of personal hygiene. Seems Drummond brought a camp hammock, slings it between the Humvees and sleeps like a baby, he said. Prick. I think I'll need one of your famous massages to get all of these kinks out. <wink>
Love you
N

P.S. had to pull Ramirez off Drummond, seems the guy has no boundaries. Asshole.

Day 22

Finally back at my CHU, who knew I would miss a metal box so much. I swear I showered for an hour. Probably not, but God, it felt good. The dust is everywhere here; sometimes I think I'm a dust magnet. Feels like I've eaten a ton of it. Now I remember why I don't like camping. Hope Grace is staying away from the Timmy kid.
Forever my love,
N

Claire closed the journal, her finger between the pages. Something was didn't seem right. Nic sounded...depressed, distant, unhappy with the assignment. The man she was working with sounded like an asshole, but Claire could only judge from what Nic had written. Perhaps the journal entries to come would shed more light on what was going on. She remembered when someone interrupted them a few times. That someone had to be the Drummond person she was referring to in the entries. Ramirez...Claire wondered what happened to her in the explosion.

Claire walked the hall in front of Nic's room, pacing back and forth, reading further in Nic's journal. Her heart felt like it would collapse at some of the things Nic had to endure. Nights spent sleeping in a Humvee. No shower for days. Wet wipes her only means of hygiene. These things would make most women scream, but Nic wrote about them as casually as she did mentioning the weather, only the weather was hell. Her admiration only grew for her wife as she continued to read the entries, and then she came to the final entries just before the explosion that had injured her. Nic knew something was up; she could feel it and said as much in her journal. Claire paused as she started to read what would be Nic's final entry. She wanted to wait to read that last entry; the build-up had been coming. Her heart quickened at the thought Nic had found out what exactly Drummond was up to. She all but eluded to it in the post before the last one. Did she want to know what Nic knew? Would it taint her view of the Marine Corps and how they had treated her wife? She suspected so. She closed the journal and slipped it back into the manila envelope, saving it for later when she and Nic could talk about what had happened to cause the explosion.

Nurses on their rotations stopped every once

in a while and offered to get her coffee. She'd asked for information on Nic, but none was forthcoming. They only said that the doctor would be out when the surgery was over and brief her. Checking her watch, she saw it was already eight-thirty and still no word. She wanted to walk down to the recovery waiting room, but she was afraid Nic would be upset seeing her there. So, she waited in Nic's room. She didn't want anything affecting Nic's post-op care and a pissed off Nic would affect Nic's post-op care. She'd thought about what the doctor had said about Nic not wanting her in Germany. It shocked her actually, but Nic was proud and being less than one-hundred percent was unacceptable in Nic's book. She was hard on herself, while she was understanding and compassionate with others. So she would wait patiently for Nic to come out of surgery. Opening the leather clad journal, she slipped the strip of leather from the place it had been holding and continued to read what could only be described as Nic's raw thoughts on her mission. It scared Claire that Nic had to endure some of the shitty behavior of an unprofessional civilian, but Claire was sure Nic didn't know how spot on she was when she said he would get them killed. Luckily for the crew, he was the only casualty; karma had exacted its amount due that day.

A squeaking and beeping made Claire turn around. Coming down the hallway was an intern pushing a gurney, and Doctor Morton, still in his scrubs. Nic was propped up, asleep. Half of her face was bandaged, and the other half didn't look much better. She was hooked up to an IV and heart monitor. Claire raced up to the gurney and grabbed Nic's good hand.

"How did she do, Dr. Morton?"

"She did great, it was a little touch-and-go there for a minute. Her blood pressure dropped and I thought we might lose her. She's been through a lot, so we just need to give her time."

Lose her. Was he saying that Nic almost died on the operating table? Oh God, she hadn't even had a chance to talk to Nic and she almost died. No, no, no. This couldn't be happening to them. This just couldn't be happening. She clutched Nic's hand tighter, bringing it up to her lips and kissing it. Smoothing Nic's hair out of her face, she bent down and kissed her cheek. She wasn't going anywhere, that was all there was to it. Wherever Nic was, Claire was there, too.

"Okay, let me call another attendant and we'll get Nic on her bed and comfortable." Dr. Morton patted Claire on the back.

Within the hour, Nic was on her bed and appeared to be resting comfortably. Pulling up the chair, Claire clutched Nic's hand as if it was her only lifeline. She would be awake soon and Claire wasn't sure which Nic would show up when she found out Claire was there. She'd worry about that later; right now, she was just happy to be with Nic.

Chapter Twenty-two

Without thinking, Nic tried to open her mouth, but couldn't. God, she felt like she'd been hit by a mack truck. Something warm grasped her hand and when she pulled away, she heard someone gasp.

"Nic?"

She had to be dreaming again, because the voice sounded just like Claire's, but Claire was thousands of miles away with Grace. Her medications were screwing with her and she realized life sucked sometimes.

"Nic?"

Closing her eyes, she just hoped that the medications would give her dreamless sleep, yet dreams of Claire plagued her. Her movement was limited. Her right side was so damaged it would be months before she could sleep on that side and she was a right-sided sleeper. Running her tongue across her teeth, she felt the empty hole of two missing teeth. Lucky for her they were to the side and not directly in front. Somehow it didn't matter to her; she was happier to be alive than worried about a few missing teeth. As she assessed her injuries, she found it was clear that her right side had taken the brunt of the damage. Funny, it was the first time she was actually clear enough to check herself out. Moving her right arm, she felt the constriction of her wrappings. Her ribs protested at the movement so she stopped.

"Nic?" There it was again, Claire's voice. Obviously she was dreaming and not as awake as she thought.

"Nic honey, can you open your eyes?"

Barely able to peel her dry eyelids open, she squinted at the bright lights.

"Let me get the lights," Claire's voice said.

The lights dimmed and Nic pried them open a tad more. Searching the room, her gaze landed on someone sitting in the chair on her left. Trying to focus with one eye, she barely could make out the blonde hair and smile of her wife.

"Claire? What...."

A finger covered Nic's lips, stopping her from speaking.

"Save your strength, honey. I'm right here if you need me. Try and get some sleep. You're just barely out of surgery and the doctor said it was touch-and-go for a minute. Rest, I'll be here if you need me."

Soft warm lips covered hers, the lingering kiss sending her to dreamland.

"Sergeant. Get your ass up." Nic screamed at the body lying on the ground. Bending over, she tried to pull Ramirez with her right hand but it wouldn't work, so she grabbed the battle gear with her left and pulled Ramirez towards the side of the road. Arching back, she let the weight of her body work to get Ramirez out of the fire. The Humvee was smoking and a small fire was licking through into the compartment. It wouldn't be long before it was completely engulfed and with all that ammunition in the back, it would turn into a Chinese New Year parade. Nic looked over at Drummond, or what was left of him, lying in front of the Humvee. His

lower torso was gone, and from the hips up, he was a mass of frayed flesh. Blood was oozing from his nose and open mouth and his eyes...he was staring into nothingness.

"Christ."

Nic hobbled back to Ramirez and pulled the mic on her radio.

Keying the mic a couple of times, she tried to get someone on the other end, but it was dead. Looking back, she could see a couple of soldiers scrambling to recover their own men.

"Fuck."

She grabbed Ramirez's battle vest and pulled her again towards the road. Suddenly the Humvee exploded and the percussion tossed Nic and Ramirez back into the ditch that ran alongside the road. Spitting something out of her mouth, she felt her stomach heaving. Turning on her side, she puked whatever she'd had for breakfast that day.

"Ramirez," she said, crawling to the lifeless body. As she pushed herself, a commotion broke out on the dirt road above them. Something inside Nic made her cover Ramirez with her own body and lay still. She could hear Ramirez fight for every breath; slow shallow breathing and a gurgling sound every once in a while was all Ramirez could push.

Men were yelling above her, in a language she didn't understand. Footsteps came closer...more yelling and someone grabbed Nic and turned her over and poked at her. Her only thought was to lay still and play dead.

"This bitch is dead. And the other one under her is too." He kicked Nic in the ribs so hard she felt them break. The pain was excruciating, but she didn't move.

Ramirez was barely breathing, laying motionless, blood oozing from her mouth, her ears, and her nose. If she wasn't dead, she soon would be if Nic didn't do something. Waiting, she kept her eyes closed. The sounds of gunfire rang out above her, as the men who had kicked her ran for cover.

"Shoot those mother fuckers." A male voice screamed as he ran past her. His English was perfect. She barely caught a glimpse of sand colored boots running past her as more automatic fire was laid down past them.

Nic tried to sit up when she heard someone call out to her. "Colonel, don't move. We've got a medic on the way," a soldier said, pushing her back down on the desert floor.

"Don't worry about me, check Ramirez, she isn't moving."

"We'll take care of her, ma'am. Lie still and try not to move. You're pretty banged up yourself." He smiled down at her. "Medic, get your ass over here, we have wounded."

His screaming voice was the last thing she remembered before she passed out.

※※※※

Claire felt helpless as Nic twitched and groaned. Claire rubbed her hand and then lifted it to her lips, placing a kiss on each bruised knuckle. She'd never seen anyone as battered at Nic. She wasn't allowed to see Mike at the burial, so she imagined he looked worse than Nic; he'd died of his injuries.

Standing, she walked to the doorway and stretched. She hadn't eaten and was wondering if she had time to catch a bite while Nic slept. A nurse came to the door and looked at Claire.

"Are you okay?" She said, offering a polite smile.

"I'm fine, thanks. How long do you think Nic will stay a sleep?"

"Probably most of the day. She still has her catheter in, but once that comes out we're going to want to get her up and walking."

"But she's just had surgery. Surely you can't expect her to get up already." Claire was incensed that they would want Nic up so soon. She'd been through hell and now they wanted to add to her pain and misery.

"We find that the sooner a patient is up and moving, the more quickly they recover. We aren't going to have her running or anything, but we do want to reduce the possibility of blood clots, bed sores, and a lot of other problems that come with being in a bed too long."

"I see."

"Don't worry, Mrs. Caldwell, she's in good hands. I promise." The nurse tried to sound reassuring, but Claire wasn't buying it.

"I'm sure she is, I didn't mean to imply that you didn't know what you're doing, it just seems… well I'm just worried about my wife. I'm sure you can understand."

"Of course. If you want to get a bite to eat, I'm going to be taking her vitals, and taking her catheter out. You may not want to be around for that and it would save the colonel some embarrassment."

"Thank you, I'll grab something quick and be right back." Claire grabbed her wallet out of her purse, her sweater, and left Nic in the capable hands of the nurse.

Walking through certain parts of the hospital was like walking through a battlefield. Men and some women were in various states of injury. One man hobbled past Claire on two prosthetic legs, while another sat in a wheelchair missing every limb but his left arm. He sat facing the window watching the lawn being mowed, and when it was done, the man mowing the lawn waved at the man in the wheelchair. Clearly he'd been here a while if the gardener knew him. As he moved his electric wheelchair past Claire, she notice severe burns to his face and neck. She squirmed at the condition of the poor man. Getting on the elevator, she waited as another soldier struggled to get his legs to move forward and get on the elevator. He moved his crutches forward and then swung his hips to move his legs. One and then the other pivoted as he slowly made his way on.

"Second floor please," he said, looking ahead.

"Cafeteria?" Claire questioned, trying to make small talk.

"Beats the food they serve in the rooms. Besides, I need my exercise." He smiled without looking at Claire.

A thin robe covered shorts and an Army T-shirt. The shorts exposed his prosthetic legs that had running shoes on them.

"Do you mind if I ask what happened?" The look he gave her surprised Claire. "I'm sorry, it's none of my business."

"No, I've just never had anyone ask me what happened. It's not like people here don't already have their own baggage. I mean everyone's basically coming from the same place. Well, almost everyone."

He finally looked at her and did a quick visual up and down her body.

"My spouse is here."

"Oh wow, you came all the way around the world just to be with your husband. Must be nice." Claire couldn't miss the bitterness that laced his voice.

"My first husband was killed in Iraq and I didn't want Nic to die alone if that was a possibility."

"I'm sorry for your loss, I didn't mean to imply anything, it's just I haven't seen my wife for a while."

"How long have you been here?"

"Ah, about a month. I get to go home—well, at least stateside at the end of the week. More PT, physical therapy, at Walter Reed and I'm hoping my wife can get there, but we have three kids and it's hard to get from Kentucky to D.C."

The elevator dinged and the door slid open. Claire held the door while the young man swung his way out of the elevator. They both moved towards the tray holder and Claire let the soldier go first.

"What's your name?" Claire said, placing a tray in behind his.

"Chett Burbone." He smiled. He must have known what was coming next.

"Hmm, interesting, Kentucky, bourbon—you must get all sorts of grief about that." Claire returned the warm smile.

"Yeah, a little," he said, squeezing his fingers together. "I'd love a little bourbon right about now." He pushed his tray further down, filling it to the point Claire wondered if he was going to be able to eat all that food.

Checking out, Claire looked at his tray and then hers and offered to carry his. "Here, let me get that. I'd hate to see all that food go to waste on the floor."

"Thanks, I guess I was hungrier that I thought."

"I think it was the carrot cake," Claire ribbed him, noticing he had two pieces on his plate.

"Yes, ma'am, it's been a while since I've had a good dessert."

Placing their trays on a table, she pulled a chair out for him and then took the chair opposite.

"Oh, I'm sorry, is it all right if I sit with you?"

"Please, it's been a while since I talked to anyone other than some doctor, nurse, or someone in military." He motioned to the seat.

Sitting was another slow process for Chett. He had to pull the chair out far enough to sit and then swing his legs under the table. Hopping the chair forward, he was almost under, but still pretty far from his plate, so Claire pushed the round table towards him.

"Thanks, I'm still trying to get used to maneuvering with these things."

He clasped his hands bowed his head and started to say grace over his plate.

Claire bowed her head out of respect and waited to eat.

"Thank you, God, for this food, help it to nourish our bodies, may your words be a nourishment for our souls. Grant us safe travels as we move through this world. Amen."

Claire looked down at her food and waited for Chett to begin digging through his food. She wondered how a man who'd lost both legs still believed in God. Earlier, she'd cursed God for Nic's injuries and now she sat with a man whose injuries were twice as bad as Nic's and yet he still loved God. He hadn't lost his faith.

"So Chett, what's home like?"

Chewing a little faster he tried to speak around his food, but put his finger up asking Claire to wait a moment.

"Pardon me." He swallowed. "Home is beautiful, my wife is beautiful, my kids are just awesome. I can't wait to get home to see them, but I want to walk to them without these things," he said, pointing to the crutches leaning against the table.

"Have the doctors said how long that will take?" Claire was interested in why a man would wait to see his kids and wife for that long.

"About another month."

"Your wife can't get to D.C., huh?"

"Oh, no, she can get there. It'd take some planning and all, but I don't want her there. I don't want her to see me like this." He slowed down his eating and pushed around a piece of broccoli. He suddenly seemed to lose his appetite.

"I'm sorry, I didn't mean to—"

"Oh, no, ma'am, it's just that I walked out on two good legs, I want to walk back to them, maybe not on my own legs, but I want to walk back under my own power. I don't want her to see me like this." He swept his hands down his body.

"I just can't bear to see the pity in her eyes that I know is coming. I want to be the same husband I was when I left. I'm hoping they find me a duty station where I can continue to be a soldier."

"Really? After everything you've been through." Claire was shocked.

"I know you may not understand this, ma'am, but I've wanted to be a soldier my whole life and I'm not going to let an IED change that. I'll have to admit it's in the Army's hands, but I'm hopeful they find a place for me."

Claire hoped Nic was done with the Marine Corps. While she understood this young man's desire to serve, Claire wondered what she would find when she was finally able to talk to Nic. A Marine ready to go back, or a Marine ready to turn the page to a new chapter of her life. She was being selfish, she knew it, but she was sure this soldier's wife might have a different opinion when she saw him.

"I'm sure they will, Chett. They need dedicated men like you to serve."

"Just like your husband, too, I'm sure." He shoveled a huge piece of carrot cake in his mouth and moaned at its goodness. "Sorry."

"No worries, enjoy it. You've more than deserved it."

Studying the young man, she only had one selfish thought. God, she was lucky Nic wasn't injured as badly.

Chapter Twenty-three

Nic reached up to untighten the band that was constricting her head. She couldn't take the pressure anymore and just wanted it to stop. The only problem was there wasn't a band there. Forcing her eyes open, she searched for the button that would hopefully bring her some sort of relief.

"Yes, Colonel," someone said through the speaker on her bed rail. "What can I get for you?"

"Somfing for sis pain, plees." Nic said barely above a whisper.

"Colonel, are you pressing your pain button?"

God, what a stupid question. *Of course* she was pressing her pain button. Wasn't she? Feeling around she tried to search for the button connected to the morphine drip but it wasn't under her hand. Christ, she needed to clear her medically induced fog.

"Pee," she blurted out.

"That's a good sign, Colonel. If you're in a hurry, you can release your bladder, you still have your catheter in—"

"I'll remove it myseff," Nic said.

"No, no, no, we'll be right there to help you. Sit still for just a minute and someone will be there to remove it so you can go to the bathroom, Colonel."

"Fine," Nic said, more indignant than she knew why. Talking was an excursion she couldn't afford at the moment. It took all of her energy to try to be understood. She still sounded like a drunken sailor still on a bender.

Within a minute, a nurse was bedside and pulling the coverings back, exposing Nic to anyone who might happen to walk in.

"Captain," Nic said, pushing her gown down.

"Colonel," the nurse said, trying to peel the blanket back. "If you'd like to get up to go to the bathroom, then we need to take this out."

"Here?" she groaned.

The nurse looked around the room and then back at Nic. "Would you prefer a male nurse to do this? I'll understand if you're uncomfortable." She put the blanket back and stepped away.

Nic grabbed the pen, wrote another note, and twisted around.

"What? No, no, I don't want a male nurse, somewhere less visible than—" the nurse looked at Nic. "Less visible than your own private room? Are you expecting your platoon to come in for a visit? 'Cause otherwise there isn't anywhere more private than this, Colonel." She put her hand on her hip, curled her lip, and rolled her eyes. The only thing missing was a sigh.

Then she sighed, still looking at Nic.

"Really, Colonel?"

"Sorry." Nic pulled the blanket back and said, "Get over, peese," she said. Her jaw ached as she tried to move it to talk. She felt like a little kid and the best she could do was grunt out a response.

The indignity of it all, Nic thought as the thin line passed easily out of her. The only thing missing was having someone walk in. The curtain swayed as it was parted and Claire walked in just as the nurse was placing a gauze on Nic's urethra. She dropped the blanket back over Nic's legs and looked up, eyebrows raised in surprise.

"Oh...oh uhm...sorry, I didn't know you were awake already. I can come back when you're done," Claire said, her face coloring in embarrassment.

Nic hadn't been dreaming - Claire really was here in Germany. She wasn't sure how she felt at the moment, seeing Claire in the flesh. The inner turmoil churned in her gut, and her pride pricked as she realized Claire had seen her at probably her worst. The bruising, the scars, and the broken bones were nothing compared to how Nic saw herself at that moment. She could barely walk, she couldn't talk, she couldn't hear out of her right ear, and she didn't know if she would lose sight in her right eye. To say she was a mess was the biggest understatement. Nic turned her face away from Claire and looked at the nurse who was disposing of the bag and catheter and washing her hands. She'd wait to say anything until the nurse was done; besides, she didn't know what to say to her wife.

Claire sat in the chair next to her bed and rested her hand on Nic's leg. Nic felt her rubbing her fingertips back and forth across her thigh, probably the only thing that wasn't battered on Nic. Without a thought, Nic started to cry. She couldn't stop herself. The anguish of Claire seeing her like this was more than she could bear. She sucked in a breath that made the nurse and Claire turn and stare at her. Without missing a beat, the nurse yanked a few tissues from the box, handed them to Nic, and swung the rail down.

"Okay, Colonel, I'm ready when you are," the nurse said, helping Nic swing her legs to the floor.

Nic swooned as she sat up. The last thing she wanted was to look weak in front of Claire. Suddenly, she didn't need to go to the bathroom. She waved the nurse off.

"No," Nic whispered.

"No bathroom, or no help? I'm not letting you walk by yourself to the bathroom Colonel." The nurse's tone made it clear she wasn't going to be pushed off.

"No bafroom."

"Are you sure?"

Nic nodded and tried to lift her legs. They wouldn't budge. So the nurse lifted Nic back into bed and pulled the blanket over her.

"Call me when you're ready to go to the bathroom. No trying to get there on your own, Colonel."

Nic nodded and then let a groan slip just as the nurse exited the room.

"What's wrong? Are you in pain?" Claire came around the bed and gently cradled Nic's left hand. "I love you so much, please don't make me leave," Claire said, her lips quivering. She gently laid herself across Nic's lap and started sobbing. Nic was crushed. That was exactly what she had wanted to tell Claire. She didn't want Claire to see her like this and now she had. Nic needed to decide what was more important, having the comfort of her wife or her need to be seen as that strong and capable woman who had walked out on her own strength only a few months earlier. Nic let her fingers glide through Claire's hair. She lost herself in the mindless stroking, a thought to another day, alone with her wife in the backyard. The day they'd made love and promises to keep each other safe. How could Nic have made that promise, a promise she'd broken to the woman who mattered most. She hoped Claire would forgive her, but looking down at her other hand, the cast weighing her down, Nic doubted she could forgive herself for what had happened.

Nic's tears streamed down her face; she couldn't stop them anymore. Clearing her throat, she drew Claire's attention. Making a writing motion, she looked at the pad and pen on her side table and motioned at it with her chin.

"This?" Claire picked it up.

"Pees." Was the best Nic could do. Her mouth ached, her jaw was swollen, and she was finally coming out of the fog of the surgery. Scribbling with her left hand, she passed the pad to Claire.

"How long have I been here?" Claire questioned.

Nic nodded. She had so many questions, but she doubted she would last long enough to ask them all. Maybe the doctor has shared more with Claire than he had with her.

"I got here late two nights ago. The day before you had surgery." Claire wiped at the tears smudging her mascara in the corners. She still looked beautiful to Nic, no matter what. "How's the pain?"

Nic teetered her hand back and forth. It was manageable at the moment.

"Would you like some water?"

Nic offered a small smile and nodded her head.

Claire held the water cup while Nic took a sip and then pulled back. Nic picked up the pen and scribbled again. Passing the pad to Claire, she waited expectantly.

"Food?" Nic nodded again; they were doing well considering Nic wasn't left-handed. "I'll talk to the nurse. How long has it been since you've eaten?"

Nic couldn't remember the last time she'd had something to eat. Afghanistan was probably the last place she'd had a meal. Liquids were about the only thing she could remember since arriving.

She shrugged.

"I'll get the nurse. How do they expect you to get any better if you don't eat? You need to eat and get your strength back. I'll find that nurse and get you something to eat." Claire dabbed at her eyes, straightened her blouse, and turned towards Nic.

Cupping Nic's face in her hands, she looked down at Nic's lips and then at her good eye. Nic could tell she was fighting back tears. For a brief moment, Nic saw pity and then it was gone.

"I love you no matter what. I don't care if you have no arms, no legs, have lost all your teeth, I want to spend the rest of my life with you." Gently, Claire placed a kiss on her lips, lingering before she pulled away and smiled. "How does a milkshake sound?"

Nic could only smile as more tears fell. Wiping at Nic's face, Claire kissed her again and then brushed her face against the side of Nic's. The warm soft skin sent a shiver through her. *At least I'm still alive*, Nic thought, her heart racing.

Cupping Claire's hand in her own, she lifted it to her lips, turned Claire's hand over, and kissed her palm. It was a gesture Nic used when she wanted to be intimate with Claire. They had their own language when it came to love and now seemed like as good a time as any to use it, especially since she had a tough time speaking.

"Colonel...I'm surprised at your boldness," Claire chided.

A sheepish look was all Nic could pull off. She wasn't much for playing coy, but Claire on the other hand, Claire could make Nic's heart skip a beat just with a flutter of her eyelashes as she dropped them demurely.

Nic shook her head, she didn't want Claire to get the wrong idea.

"I know, baby, I know." Claire kissed Nic's only bare cheek and whispered, "You shouldn't tease like that, it gets me hot."

Claire turned and left without looking at Nic. Good thing, her cheeks were on fire and she was a little more than embarrassed by her own actions.

Chapter Twenty-four

Claire made a quick trip past the nurse's station and stopped to talk to the nurse she'd seen earlier with Nic.

"Captain, may I have a word?" Claire asked.

"Of course, Mrs. Caldwell. What can I do for you?" she said, wrapping a stethoscope around her neck and pocketing the round end into her pocket.

"Captain, I'd like your honest assessment of my wife's condition. When can I take her home?"

"Ma'am, I'm not the doctor–"

"I understand that, but you've been working with Nic since she's arrived, right?"

"True."

"So what's your honest assessment? I want to take her home as soon as possible, but I don't want to rush her. If I ask her, she'll tell me she's ready to go now."

"She can't leave now, Mrs. Caldwell. She's just had surgery to repair her orbital socket and we don't know what the results of that surgery will be. She could lose some vision, she might lose all of her vision in that eye. We just don't know yet. As for her other injuries, she is permanently deaf in her right ear, and given her physical condition before her accident, her broken bones will heal quickly."

"What about mentally?"

"I'm not a shrink. I just heal the physical not the

mental." The nurse gently grabbed Claire's forearm and pulled her out of the path of traffic around the station. "I've seen lots of patients like your wife. Some do well, they never need help beyond their broken bones, but I read Colonel Caldwell's medical file, she's been injured before...lost everyone. Can I give you some advice? Off the record?"

"Sure." Worry creased Claire's face. She knew what was coming, but how would she convince Nic she needed to see someone, especially this time?

"When you get home, get Colonel Caldwell to talk to someone. She may not think she needs to now, but eventually the nightmares will keep her up. She won't sleep, she'll think she's handling it, but she'll just be going through the motions."

"How—"

The nurse lifted her sleeve back and exposed herself to Claire. Claire covered her mouth before she could let out a gasp. A withered arm, badly burnt to the elbow, almost made Claire faint.

"Oh God, what happened?" she said without thinking, "I sorry, I just—"

Rolling her sleeve back into place, the nurse looked around and just smiled pleasantly. "I was on my way to a hospital in Afghanistan that was bombed. I was lucky..."

Claire thought about the young man in the cafeteria, and now the nurse. She'd imagined the story replayed itself with regularity at the hospital, but it still shook her to the core. They were all still alive, serving, or wanting to serve even with injuries that most of society would shrink away from and yet here they were a testament to perseverance, courage, and duty. Nic would be one of these...what was the word she was looking for...it didn't matter. Nic *was* one of them.

Lowering her head somewhat, Claire felt shameful, for *what* she didn't know. She suspected it was because she was healthy, walking on her own, or just unblemished. She didn't belong to this long line of courageous soldiers. She was only a wife, here to bring back her spouse, and now she felt guilty for being here.

"Can I bring you anything from the cafeteria?" She muttered, barely able to look at the captain.

"I'm good, thanks. Look, I didn't show you that to make you uncomfortable."

"No, I know...I'm not, really," Claire tried to sound convincing, but she was failing miserably.

"I just want you to be prepared for the person you're going to be bringing home."

"Thank you, I appreciate that."

"Well, if you'll excuse me I have rounds and a couple of stubborn patients who don't like to take their medicines."

"Captain?"

"You can call me Anne."

A rather plain name for such a good-looking woman, Claire thought. "Thank you, Anne. I was just wondering, how badly would I be breaking the rules if I brought Nic back a milkshake?"

Anne pursed her lips and gave Claire a look that would wither any soldier and then she relaxed. "I won't be doing rounds on her floor for another hour, so if the evidence is gone by then...just don't let her have too much. She's on a restricted diet with her jaw wired and I would hate to have her throw up."

"Understood and thank you, for everything."

Claire touched her arm.

Patting Claire's hand, she smiled and turned to finish her rounds without saying anything.

Claire was definitely an interloper in a world she was only just now starting to understand.

≈≈≈≈

Nic laid in her bed. She wasn't one to sleep on her back so the urge to turn over was like an itch that she couldn't reach, she just couldn't do it. The nurse had offered to give her something so she could sleep, but she'd turned it down. It would still be there later if she changed her mind, she'd been told.

Dim light seeped under the partially opened door. The quiet of the ward made her anxious, but she didn't know why. Perhaps it was because she couldn't just get up when she wanted to, or maybe it was the fact that she couldn't sleep. Every once in a while, the squeak of rubber soles on a polished floor made her look at the door, waiting for someone to come in, yet the person just walked passed her door. The squoosh/phit of the ventilator and the beep of heart monitor next door were a constant. It just wasn't as noticeable during the day when people were milling about the floor.

With the exception of the hourly rounds the nurses did, Nic was all alone. Just watching TV fatigued her to the point that it was useless to try and even watch and reading was out of the question, so what did someone like Nic do?

Remember.

It was the side effect of injury. Trying to remember what happened and if she could have done something different. Could she have prevented Max's death? Hell, did she want to prevent the prick's death? The fact that Ramirez was right, he was CIA, was beside the point. He was using them as cover to find out information about a new terrorist group, an offshoot of the Taliban. The bastard had acted like it was every day the CIA used soldiers for cover.

"Look Colonel, it doesn't matter now. You're here and I'm in charge, so unless you have higher connections than I do, I suggest you get used to it and do your job," the smug bastard had said one afternoon when they'd been out interviewing tribal leaders.

"Does the Commandant know you're using Marines and soldiers to do your dirty work?" Nic wanted to pinch his head off, but Ramirez was standing off her shoulder and she was an officer. Anything less than professional wouldn't be tolerated, even for her.

"How did you find out?" Drummond said, leafing through some notes he was transcribing.

"Does it matter?"

"Well, it does if you were going through my personal things." He looked up at her and then at Ramirez. "I bet it was you, wasn't it?"

"Excuse me?" Ramirez gripped her rifle and started to raise it.

"No, actually it was me. I was handed a communication for you, it slipped out of my hands and flew all over the desert. By the time I retrieved it, I read a few lines. I have an eyes-only clearance, so your shit is safe with me. But why lie? Why not just get assigned—"

"We don't have time to get clearance, a squad set up, and then wait two years before D.C. jumps on this. I called in a favor from NPS and bam, here you are."

"Commander Jackson is in on this?" On one hand,

Nic was surprised, but then again he hated her and this made perfect sense. He'd bounced her right out of her research position and gotten rid of her all in one swift flick of a pen. Bastard.

"We go way back, Annapolis if you must know. I needed a favor and my brother helped me out. He knows how regulations can sometimes impede what's best for the—"

"Oh, and you're the arbitrator of what's best for the United—"

"Yes," he said, cutting Ramirez off. "If a few unknowns get killed in Afghanistan, no one is the wiser. So goes the game of war."

"So we're expendables." Nic was getting madder by the minute. Pompous asshole. Black Ops shit. The government disavows any knowledge if the mission goes south and no one was the wiser. Now what?

"Well, aren't we all?" he said smugly. "If we're all lucky, we make it home in one piece. You go back to your wretched lives and I go back and—"

"Fuck you," Nic said. The only thing she wanted to do was knock his teeth out, but they were out in the desert alone and every person was important to the mission and the mission was getting back to the FOB in one piece.

Nic could see Ramirez lower her hand to the trigger guard of her rifle. Locking eyes with Ramirez, she shook her head. Ramirez slid her hand down and grabbed the pistol grip on the 240. Nic swore she could hear Ramirez's teeth clenching.

"Well, you aren't exactly my type, Colonel, but the sergeant over there, she's a—"

Ramirez pulled her fist back and let it roll right across his chin before Nic could grab her and pull her off Drummond.

"Knock it off," Nic ordered.

"You're going to pay for that, bitch. I'll see you busted down to a PFC and spending the rest of your tour in the brig."

Nic stepped between the two, realizing that whatever pull he had to get this mission approved, she was sure he could do what he threatened.

"You're going to get us all killed, you piece of shit," Ramirez spit out.

"You need to stop, soldier," Nic whispered in her ear. Whatever was eating Ramirez was like a bomb that's fuse had just been lit. She didn't want to see anything happen to Ramirez, she was a good soldier, but this was beyond a little disagreement. "Let's get going, the FOB is still a half-day's drive, and we're burning daylight."

She pushed Ramirez towards the Humvee and whispered to Ramirez.

"We'll see what DC says when we get back, so cool it."

That had been their last conversation before everything exploded.

Chapter Twenty-five

Claire's quick trip through the food line was halted when she spotted Chett sitting alone at a table, shoveling food in again.

Wow, what an appetite, she thought, watching him practically inhaling food.

"Hey, Chett, that must be some physical therapy," she said, peering at the quickly disappearing food. A few small dessert dishes were empty around the plate of food.

"Oh hey, how are you?" Chett motioned towards the chair across from him. "How's your husband doing?"

Claire's brain stuttered for a moment, trying to remember if she'd corrected him the last time they spoke. It didn't matter, it wasn't germane to their previous conversation.

"Good, how are you? Any news on when you're going home?"

Stopping mid-pass, his quick smile faded and he put his fork down. "No, not yet. Seems they are watching an infection in my stump," he said, pointing to his left leg.

"Oh, I hope it isn't anything serious."

"Naw, just being careful, I guess." He started eating again. "Whatcha got there?" He pointed to the Styrofoam cup.

"Oh, this? This is for Nic. Wired jaw, can't have

solid food." She purposely left out any pronouns.

"Oh, poor bastard." He grimaced. "I don't know what I would do if I couldn't eat. Wow, that sucks."

"Yeah, so I thought I'd get a milkshake. At least it's liquid."

"He's lucky to have you here. I mean, I would love to see my wife and kids, I just need to get well quick. Know what I mean?"

"Yeah, I do." Claire stood and pushed her chair in, slung her purse over her shoulder, and smiled at the young face.

"Careful there, you're gonna lose your package." Chett pointed to the manila envelope teetering precariously out of her purse.

"Oh, thanks. I don't want to lose that." Claire stuffed the envelope holding Nic's journal deep into her oversized purse. "Well, I don't want to keep you and I need to get this back before it melts," she said, then laughed at the thought of a melted milkshake.

"Yeah, it might go down too easy and where's the fun in a warm milkshake?" Chett waved her off and focused back on his food. "Catcha around."

"Take care."

"You too."

Claire thought about Chett all the way back to Nic's room. It sounded like he'd been here a while and an infection had to be serious, especially on a stump that would be raw from use. She hoped for his wife's sake that the infection was short-lived. If she were his wife, she would be worried sick. God, how did the families of wounded soldiers survive living so far from their loved ones? There had to be some sort of organization that helped families, right? The military was great at caring for the soldiers when they were still in. The wives had their own support tree that went into effect when a service member was injured, but if the spouse wasn't on base, it was tougher to find a support chain. She'd experienced this first hand when Mike was killed in action. The pink bayonet was launched and wives surrounded her. This time though, she hadn't experienced that support structure. It was night and day and she was only guessing, but Claire suspected it had something to do with whatever happened at the Naval Postgraduate School. There had barely been a phone call from the commandant's wife, expressing her concern over Nic's well-being. Short and sweet was the best Claire could call the brief conversation. Jordan said she was probably still pissed about the party, but no matter—Claire didn't give two flips.

Stopping at the door of Nic's room, she put her head where it needed to be, on Nic's recovery, not on some officer's wife who was as useless as tits on a boar-hog. She shook her head at the reference her dad use to say when dealing with some useless person. He didn't say much but when he did, he had a way with words.

She walked into the darkened room and heard Nic's moaning and shifting in bed.

Chapter Twenty-six

Claire reached for Nic's good hand and held it while she thrashed around in the bed. Nic had to be having a night terror. It was the only explanation Claire could come up with. Slowly, she ran her fingers through Nic's hair and whispered something only for Nic's ears. Nic stopped moving and her breathing slowed. Claire rested her head against Nic's and grimaced sympathetically at the pain her lover was obviously in. Nic turned her head towards Claire's and whispered back.

"I'm forever faithful, my love," Nic said, slurring her words through a clenched jaw.

Claire brushed her lips against Nic's; the sensation was almost illegal in Nic's condition. She craved Nic and no matter what happened to Nic, she would always be Nic's. Her mind focused at the pleading she'd offered. She knew it sounded desperate, but she didn't want to leave and Claire would do whatever it took to stay. Nic needed her, and she wanted to be needed at this very moment. She rubbed her cheek against Nic's and felt her stress decrease with each stroke. They had that effect on each other —a look, a kiss, and the world righted itself for them.

"Tell me what you need and I'll do it. I'll sleep on the floor of this room, just to be close to you. I'll move heaven and earth to help you." Claire sat on the side of Nic's bed, hesitant to touch Nic. Her body was a road map of disaster, according to the doctor. She trembled, aching to touch her lover, to let her know that she still desired Nic. No matter what happened, Claire would always be Nic's, no matter the circumstances.

"Milkshake?"

"Of course." Claire picked up the milkshake and whirled the straw around, loosening the liquid, and pressed the tip against Nic's lips. Claire's heart felt like it might break in two, the way her wife grimaced just to take a sip. Her bruised lips wrapped greedily around the straw and took a long pull.

"Slowly, my love, I don't want you to get sick."

Nic let go of the straw and rested her head back against the pillow. She let loose a sigh. A soft cough escaped and then another.

"Water?"

Nic nodded and leaned forward to take a sip.

"Small sips. Anne said you could get sick, so we should be careful." Claire pushed back at the matted hair around Nic's face. The back of her hand stroked Nic's face in comfort. "How do you feel?"

Nic rolled her eyes and barely broke a smile. "Ruff," she said before she let her left hand slide along Claire's thigh. "Mmm, sorry." Her voice cracked as she looked down at the cast and rolled it over, pushing it on to the bed.

"Sorry? What do you have to be sorry for, Nic?"

Nic motioned to her face and then her right side. "This." She still didn't look at Claire. Pushing her head back into the pillow, she turned away from Claire. Nic sucked in a breath as she softly started to sob.

"Nic?"

Nic didn't respond. She closed her eyes and refused to look at Claire, so Claire walked to the other side of the bed.

"Nichole," Claire said, her hand on her hip and the milkshake in the other hand. "This isn't your fault, so stop. There are people in here worse than you. You'll walk again, some won't." Claire reached for Nic, but she pulled away at Claire's touch. "I know it isn't easy, well...I mean I know it hurts, but I'm here for you, I'm not going away...I don't want to go away...I mean..." Claire teared up. "You don't want me to go away...do you?"

Nic clutched Claire's hand and squeezed it. Claire raised it to her lips and kissed the scarred knuckles.

"I love you," she eked out as she laid her head against Nic's chest. "I love you."

Chapter Twenty-seven

Visiting hours were over and Claire left begrudgingly. Nic rubbed the scrawled words on the pad.

She'd practically begged Claire to go back to quarters and get some rest. She supposed she could have asked the nurse to say something, but that would have embarrassed Claire. She was exhausted, her stomach was rolling from the milkshake, and the permanent headache she had was throbbing worse than ever. Nic had tried to stay off the morphine for as long as she could, grunting through the pain. She wanted to be awake as long as Claire was around, but between the pain and the excursion of being awake she'd pushed herself too far and now she had to pee.

Great.

The nurse had told her to ring for help if she needed to go to the bathroom, but she could handle a bathroom run. Claire was right; she still had her legs and her arms. She'd survived whatever had happened to her and she was strong, she was a Marine and she wasn't going to depend on someone just to go to the bathroom. It was three feet away for God's sake.

When her helicopter crashed in Iraq, she'd fought for her life, pulling herself from under the exhaust system that had pinned her to the ground. Getting off the bed would be easier than that, she just needed to think about getting off the bed. Looking down her right side, she realized her whole right side was almost unmovable. Raising the head of her bed, she sat almost upright; so far so good. Slow deep breaths, she focused on the simple task of moving the covers off. Flipping half of the side rail of the bed down, she swung a leg off. She tried to touch the floor but she was still too high. Lowering the bed, she felt her foot flatten on the floor. Pushing with her foot, she scooted towards the edge of the bed, swung her other leg over, and planted her feet firmly on the floor.

This was going to be easier than she thought. Grabbing the rail at the head of the bed, she pulled herself up and waited. She didn't have to wait long; her head swimming, she pitched forward, her right leg buckled, and she fell to her knees. Pain shot through her as everything went black. The last thing she remembered was the beeping of her heart monitor as it beat faster. *Oh, that probably wasn't good.*

❧❧❧❧

"How is momma Nic?" Grace asked.

Claire wasn't quite sure what to tell Grace. What would Nic want Grace to know? She was only six, but she was old enough to understand plenty.

"She's going to be fine, Sweetheart." That was the truth. Nic was going to be fine, eventually. "Are you being good for Auntie Jordan?"

"Yep, we went to the park and Tim's mommy was there. You should have seen Auntie Jordie. She tore her up," Grace said, and then giggled.

"Tore her up?"

"Yeah, that's what she said when Tim's mommy left. I think she was mad, 'cause she almost forgot Tim at the park."

"Hmm, can I speak to Auntie Jordan, honey?"

"Okay," Grace yelled at the phone, "Auntie Jordie, mom wants to talk to you. She's coming. When are you coming home? I miss you, mommy."

"I know sweetie, I'll be home soon. I need to help Nic get well and then we can both come home."

"Okay, tell momma Nic I love her and I hope she feels better soon so you can come home. Here's Auntie Jordie..."

With that, Grace was gone and Claire was sure she was off to terrorize the cat. *Poor kitty.*

"Hey pumpkin, how's Nic?"

"She had surgery today. They had to repair the orbital socket or she could have lost sight in her right eye. Her jaw is wired shut still and..." Claire's lip started to quiver as she tried to tell Jordan more, but she could only think about how bad Nic looked. She was so battered it scared Claire every time she looked at Nic. She couldn't help it, she started to cry again. She felt so helpless.

"Oh kitten, don't cry. Nic's strong, she's a survivor."

"You haven't seen her, Jordan. It scares me to look at her. I've never seen someone look so bad. Her face is swollen..." More tears gushed. "She's... broken...and I don't know...if my Nic is still inside... she can't talk...she's in so much pain...I...I can't..."

"Okay, calm down, honey. Take a deep breath," Jordan instructed.

Claire was finally breaking down. She'd held it all in so she could be strong for Nic, but it killed her inside to see Nic so broken.

"Let it out, honey. Just cry it all out."

"Oh...oh... God, Jor...Jordan."

"Claire, it's gonna be okay. She's alive, she's a fighter, and you and I both know that next year at this time, she's gonna be chasing Grace around and playing monster just like she did before she left."

"Jordan...she's...so—"

"I know, honey. I know. Go ahead and cry it out." Jordan tried to calm Claire but Claire was almost beside herself. She could barely breathe as she sobbed harder.

"Oh God, I can't believe I'm so out of control, Jordie."

"Honey, you've never been through something like this, so don't be so hard on yourself."

"She looks so bad."

"You need to be strong, kitten. She needs you to be her strength now. She's going to need to lean on you, sweetie. Let's just get her home and we can rally around her. We'll show her so much love she'll think she's in a harem."

"Let's rethink that, okay?" Claire sniffled.

Chapter Twenty-eight

Nic's body shook as it lay on the cold linoleum floor. She'd floated in and out of consciousness for at least the last hour. *Where were the nurses and their damn rotations?* She thought, pushing with her left hand to right herself. The heart monitor had stopped beating and had a single monotone beep, signaling she was either dead or it was disconnected from her finger. If her shivering were any indication, she wasn't dead, so it had been a while since she'd passed out. Reaching up, she tried to grab the call button on the rail, but it was up at the head of the bed. She had just enough IV line to reach to the floor, so at least her morphine drip helped keep her somewhat out of it.

If she pushed it again, she'd be down for the count again and she needed to get the hell off the floor. Gritting her teeth, she pushed off the floor and quickly reached for the sheets on the other bed. Pulling herself to a seated position, she leaned against the bed.

Arrrgghhh, she groaned, her body almost doubling over as she contorted in pain. Her breathing was labored; her head swam as blackness nibbled at the edges of her vision. Her view was tunneled and she had a hard time focusing.

A light flicked on in the room somewhere. *Finally,* she thought, trying to hold on.

"Colonel?"

"Herrr," she moaned. Her fingers were still entwined in the sheets that kept her from tumbling over.

"Colonel...geez...let me call an orderly to help you up." The captain bent down and turned Nic's chin towards her. She looked at Nic's eyes.

"No, hand," Nic said, letting go of the sheet and reaching for the nurse. "Up."

"I need to get you back into bed," said the nurse, pressing the call button. "Can you send me an orderly, please?"

"Yes, ma'am." A voice echoed over the speaker.

"Up," Nic demanded as she tried to crawl up the sleeve of the nurse.

"Let me—"

"Now." Nic's demanding tone left little choice for the nurse.

Reaching under Nic's arm and grabbing Nic's left hand, the nurse struggled to get Nic to her feet. Nic stiffened up and stood. Out of breath, she waivered but held tight to both the nurse and her resolve to stand.

"Baffwoom." Nic nodded towards her intended destination and started a slow hustle.

"Colonel, I can bring you a bedpan, I think you really should get back in bed and let me check your injuries."

"Captain," was all Nic had to say, pushing herself towards the bathroom. The captain had been in long enough to understand what Nic's measured tone and the look of death meant. Surely working with mostly injured soldiers gave her a better insight to the personal struggles many like Nic faced. Nic wasn't just proud, she was determined and wasn't ready to roll over and give up. Besides, she wasn't going to degrade herself by urinating in a bedpan if she could get to the bathroom. She couldn't explain it, but she needed to be able to take care of at least the smaller duties of taking care of herself. It was bad enough that she would probably need help disrobing and getting up and down, but she could at least have some privacy while she took care of her personal needs.

Nic leaned against the doorway of the bathroom to catch her breath. Checking out the small confines, she assessed the situation and started to maneuver closer to the toilet when the nurse's hand came around and pulled her gown around and bunched it front of her.

"Out plees," Nic didn't even look at the captain, but instead stood up and waited.

"Fine, I'll be right outside if you need me."

"Hmm."

Nic started the process of maneuvering all over again and was quite pleased with herself when she'd finally sat down. It was good thing the rail was fastened so well to the wall, since she'd practically put all of her weight on it lowering herself. Now there was only one problem, she couldn't pee. *Why?* Maybe she had performance anxiety with the nurse standing outside the door. Suddenly she could hear voices outside the bathroom door, contributing more to her panic in not being able to pee. *Really?* She rested her forehead in her palm and tried to relax. Minutes passed and she still sat waiting.

"Colonel?"

Great.

A soft knock on the door and the nurse called to her again. "Colonel? Are you okay?" The door opened and she peeked in. "Do you need help getting up?"

"No."

The nurse pursed her lips and then crinkled her nose. "Can't pee?"

Nic rolled her eyes and looked away. God, she hadn't felt this silly since she was at least five. Was there anything more embarrassing than not being able to pee? Not being able to pee on command had to be the only other humiliating time she could remember when there was a random piss test in ROTC.

"I know what will help." Before Nic could say a word, the nurse turned on the faucet and then shrugged her shoulders. "You'd be surprised how often it works." She stepped back to the door and slipped out, closing it behind her.

Seriously? Nic thought and then as if on command she started peeing. *Great, I can't believe this,* she thought, somewhat relieved. Finishing up, she pulled on the rail and hoisted herself to her feet, shuffled to the sink, and tried her best to wash her hands. Instinctively, Nic looked up into the mirror. What looked back at her shook her to her core; she was unrecognizable. One eye was a morass of colored bruises, black, blue, and shades of khaki that extended out to her cheek and to her ear. She could only imagine what her other eye looked like. She knew she would be lucky if she didn't lose sight in that eye. Nic prayed that she wouldn't, but it was clear she was deaf in her right ear; why wouldn't she lose her eyesight? Luck wasn't on her side and she needed to come to terms with the possibility she could be blind, too.

She continued to assess herself, moving closer to the mirror. Her face and lips were swollen. Lifting her upper lip, she saw the wires that kept her jaw closed and noticed two missing teeth. Christ, she was a train wreck. She tried to lift her right hand, but bandages kept her right side immobile. She could only see a few fingers that were splinted and black and blue, the bruises seeping into her palm. Her cast hid any other damage like the bandages that wrapped her face. She could only wonder what Claire's reaction was when she saw her.

She spotted the nurse, who was watching her as she studied her reflection. The pity on her face was unmistakable. Was this what the future held for her? People looking at her with pity, disgust or any other host of emotions she had no control over. Her injuries from her tour in Iraq were well hidden. No one saw them but Claire, and that had taken lots of trust and love. She turned her head away from the mirror; she couldn't stand to see how horrible she looked.

"Here, let me help with that." Nic was having a difficult time washing her hands, so the nurse washed and dried them the same way she helped Grace, like a child. "Okay, can we get you to bed now, or would you like to take a tour of the ward?"

"Phunny."

"Just checking, Colonel."

An orderly met them in the room and helped Nic onto the bed as gently as he could. It didn't matter, Nic's short excursion to the floor had taken its toll, but the psychological toll was far worse. Nic hadn't prepared herself for the sight of her reflection. How could Claire have kissed her earlier that day? Nic looked like a monster. She didn't want Claire to see her like this anymore. Claire needed to go home.

Chapter Twenty-nine

Claire grabbed two coffees at the coffee shop on the first floor, one straight black with two sugars, and one almost white. She often kidded Nic, asking her if she wanted coffee with her cream. She slipped her purse on, grabbed the cups, and elbowed her way out of the door and almost into Dr. Morton.

"Oh gosh, I'm so sorry, Dr. Morton," Claire said as she pulled the coffee cups back and nearly avoided a fatal collision with his starched white lab coat.

"Whoa, Mrs. Caldwell, how are you?" He grabbed one of the coffees as her purse slipped down her arm.

"I'm good, Dr. Morton, how are you?"

"I'm good, thank you for asking. I'm glad I bumped into you, do you have a minute?" He helped her back into the coffee shop and out of the way of a line of customers waiting.

"Of course, is everything okay?"

"I just wanted to...hmm...talk to you about something that happened earlier."

"Earlier?" Claire sat in the chair pulled out for her and eyed the doctor. Something was up and she didn't like the sudden request for a meeting. "What happened earlier? Is Nic okay?"

Dr. Morton placed his hand on Claire's and gave her a slim grin. She watched his adam's apple bob up and down as he swallowed. He was use to giving bad news so she didn't read into his behavior. In fact, she was over analyzing him; she did that when she was nervous. She watched people's reactions, their body language, and listened intently. She was an observer, Nic said. Nic told her often that she missed her calling; she should have been a shrink.

"Nic took a fall—"

"What?"

"She's okay, she's resting comfortably. She reinjured her ribs and she has some bruises, but she's okay. Seems she needed to go to the bathroom and didn't want anyone to help her. She hasn't been on her feet in almost two weeks, so it isn't uncommon for patients to get light headed the first few times they get out of bed."

"But she's going to be all right, right?" Claire felt panic flood her body. She needed to get to Nic and see that she was all right for herself.

"She's okay, but the nurse said Nic was pretty shaken up."

"I'm sure she is, if she fell the wrong way she could have really hurt herself."

"I don't think that's the only reason, seems she finally saw herself for the first time. She's requested that you not come up, right now."

"What?" Claire couldn't hide her shock. "I don't understand, I saw her earlier and she was fine, now she doesn't want to see me, why?"

Now Claire knew why the doctor was fidgeting with his watch. He's looked at it at least five times since sitting down. This wasn't the kind of news he was use to delivering, telling a spouse that their husband or wife didn't want to see them. Maybe telling someone their loved one had passed was easier. You could move on to the next patient and fix them and then they moved on to the states, never to be seen again. Superficial had its benefits, Claire suspected.

"Give her some time, Mrs. Caldwell. She's been through a lot, her body has practically been shattered, she's lost her hearing, and it's possible she could lose the sight in her eye. So she's had a lot to deal with. She lost someone in her unit, so survivor's guilt isn't out of the question, too. So imagine all of this has just hit her, she's barely out of the drug-induced coma, she finds out someone died, and she's faced with all of these injuries and is lucky to be alive and now she's finally seen what she thinks is a monster looking back at her in the mirror." He rotated his watch on his wrist. "Depression hits some people hard. So...we have to treat the whole patient, not just their injuries, but their mental state as well. I've recommended one of our psychiatrist pay her a visit."

"I don't know what to say...I mean...I just saw her." Claire sat stunned at the news. How could Nic turn her away? She was her wife.

"It isn't you, trust me. Soldiers are tough, they're the cavalry that saves the world, and they often don't think of themselves as anything but indestructible. Give her time, Mrs. Caldwell. She's struggling right now."

"But I can help her, I'm here to support her and lift her up the way she helped me when I lost someone. I just can't believe...." Claire let the words die on her lips.

"Give her some time; she needs to come to terms with what her new normal might be. She doesn't know how lucky she is, she's only seeing what's right in front of her and that's normal." Dr. Morton got up and turned to leave, but turned back around to

Claire. "Can I recommend a support group for you? You might need to be around people who are going through what you're going through."

"Thanks, I'd appreciate that. So if I walk up to see Nic, what will happen?"

"I don't know, she could freak out, she might get mad, or she could be happy to see you. I don't know. Maybe you should call first, see what she says."

Claire gave him a dubious look. Nic could barely talk and calling the room phone didn't seem like a logical answer.

"Well, I mean, perhaps you can call the nurse's station and see if they can give you an idea of her mood."

"Thanks, I'll call there first and see if I can gauge her mood."

"That might be a good idea. Please let me know if there is anything I can do. Don't worry, this too will pass."

"Thank you, Dr. Morton."

"Oh, by the way, I'm going to be taking her bandage off her right eye and checking it out. Let's hope for a positive result from the surgery."

"Of course. Thank you for the update. I'll keep my fingers crossed for a great outcome."

Claire rubbed her coffee between her palms and thought about everything the doctor told her. She would never in a million years have thought Nic would push her away. It wasn't her style, but she had gone through another life-changing event, she'd almost been killed in action again. *But she'd survived*, Claire thought. Part of her wanted to march up to Nic's room and shake her out of whatever was going on, but the shocked part of her stayed in her seat, wanting to cry.

How could Nic request that she stay away? What was she going to do now?

Claire pulled her cell phone, dialed the hospital switchboard, and requested Nic's room, but no one answered. She looked down at her watch; it was later than she thought. She waffled; should she just go up to Nic's room and act like she hadn't talked to the doctor, or should she respect Nic's wishes and wait? Anxiety raced through her. She wasn't good at waiting, not in a situation like this. Nic pushing her away scared her, but pushing Nic scared her more. Tossing the coffees in the trash, she slumped her shoulders in defeat. She'd go back to her room and wait for a phone call, but Nic was crazy if she thought she'd wait forever.

Chapter Thirty

Nic rested in the darkness of her room. Her mind raced as she thought about the ugliness of her injuries. The lack of light kept her concealed, hidden from passing eyes. She suddenly heard someone whistling down the hall and then it stopped. The door opened and a voice wafted in.

"Helloooo, Nickie? Are you awake?" the Irish accent whispered.

She ignored the inquisition. Lying in the dark gave her a sort of invisibility, as far as she was concerned, that kept her concealed and alone. Just the way she wanted it.

"Colonel?"

The voice had a familiarity, but she couldn't quite place it. Her drug-induced fog allowed her to check out when she most wanted it and now she wanted to be left alone, so she didn't engage the voice calling out to her. Her room lights flicked on and she shielded her eyes as the glare of the lights seemed to burn through her consciousness. Willing them to go off was an exercise in futility, so she pulled her covers over her head.

"Aw, there you are, Nickie."

Whoever it was seemed to know her and she was intrigued. Peeking out from under the cover, she peeled an edge down and spied a priest sitting in the chair next to her bed.

"Off," Nic commanded. "Lights...please."

"Aw, you want the lights off, no problem. If you promise to talk to me I'll be happy to oblige," the priest said, flicking the lights off. "Nickie, it's Father O'Reilly, we served together at Camp Pendleton, do you remember me?"

How could she not remember Father O'Reilly? He was the Chaplain who accompanied her on the inform that had led her to Claire. What the hell was he doing in Germany? Last she'd heard he was on the way to retirement. Pulling the cover up to just under her eyes, she tried to study the man in a collar. He'd traded in his uniform for a black suit and white collar. From what she could see, he was whiter around the temples, but none the worse for wear.

"Faffer." She could barely mouth the word, before her head slipped back against the pillow.

"Rest, Nickie...I'm not going anywhere, Nickie. I'll be here when you get up."

"Go," she said in her most commanding voice. Locked jaw and all. "Tired."

"Aye, I'm sure you are, but I would be remiss if I didn't check in on you. I saw Claire downstairs and she's a wee bit concerned that you won't see her. I hear you gals got married. Congratulations." Father O'Reilly rubbed her arm under the cover. "That's no way to treat your wife, Nickie."

Tears seeped down the sides of Nic's face. She'd told the doctor that Claire needed to stay away. She suddenly wasn't ready to have her wife see her ugly face again. It had taken Nic by surprise and now she couldn't even look at her wife, knowing this is what Claire would see for the rest of their married life.

"Why Nickie? Why won't you see your lovely

wife?" O'Reilly inquired, still rubbing her arm.

Nic couldn't take it anymore. She flipped on the light on the rail of her bed. The fluorescent light hummed behind her as she stared at Father O'Reilly. He didn't search her face, he didn't flinch, he just smiled and grabbed her hand with both of his and mouthed a prayer.

"You've taken a beating Nickie. Anyone one else hurt in the accident?" His gaze didn't stray, even though she wanted it too. She wanted him to cringe, to pull back at the sight of her. She waited for the look of pity, but nothing.

"Yes."

"Died?"

"Yes."

"I'm sorry for your loss, Nickie," he said very softly.

"Not mine," Nic corrected.

He gave her a puzzled look and then motioned to his jaw. "Wired shut?"

She nodded.

"Aw, now I understand. You were so quiet, I thought you might not want to talk."

"No," she said, pushing her pain button again and resting her head against the pillow.

She wanted to purge herself of the guilt she felt for surviving another brush with death. She wanted to tell him everything she'd done since leaving Pendleton, but now it all seemed so insignificant. Their verbal jousting had been one of the highlights of her time in San Diego. He'd become somewhat of a father figure while she worked out her feelings for Claire and now here he sat counseling her one more time.

"Nickie, it's been a while and we have some

catching up to do, so why don't you get some sleep. I'll be back and we can talk more about you, Claire, and that beautiful little girl you have waiting for you at home." He grabbed her shoulder and squeezed lightly. "I'll see you tomorrow, huh?"

Nic nodded and patted his hand. She could barely keep her eyes open. Her waking moments were longer, but more taxing. She wanted out of bed and would push herself, do whatever it took to get on her feet and back home, but suddenly she was glad to find some relief in sleep.

❧❧❦❦

"Good morning, Colonel. Sorry to wake you, but I need to get you up. So what do you say we get you to the bathroom?" a new nurse said, flipping the light switch above Nic's bed. Nic shielded her eye and looked around the room, expecting to see Father O'Reilly, only he wasn't there.

Her mouth felt like a giant cotton ball had taken up residence inside when she tried to swallow. Reaching for the cup, she slipped the straw between her lips and slowly pulled enough water to swish around her mouth and then swallow. The swelling all around her face was going down, her lips were almost back to their normal size, and she could squint her eye with little pain. She'd been religious about icing her bruises, stretching her legs, and moving what she could move even if the pain almost made her black out.

Nic picked up the pad, wrote on it, and passed it to the nurse.

"Hmm, where is Father O'Reilly? I don't know

a Father O'Reilly. Sorry." She passed the pad back to Nic.

She scribbled again and passed it back.

"He visited you last night? I'm sorry, Colonel, but there wasn't a priest on the floor last night. We call when we have to give last rites to a patient, but that's Father Nelson, he's the only Catholic priest I know for the hospital. Are you sure it wasn't him?"

Nic searched her recollection and knew it was Father O'Reilly. What was going on here? She'd heard him plain as day and surely she didn't mistake his reassuring pat on her shoulder. She scribbled again and passed it over.

"I'm sure, Colonel. I've been on all night and I didn't see anyone come in a collar. Besides, Father Nelson always stops by the nurse's station and gives us little sermon on service. Nice guy," she said, making some notations on Nic's chart and checking her vital signs. "Maybe you were dreaming, you're on morphine and it can affect people differently. I once had a patient who swore I was his mother. Unfortunately, he was about fifty-five and his mother had died twenty years earlier. Weird huh?"

Nic nodded. She was confused. Had it all been a dream? She'd never dreamt about the priest before, so it left her a little more than uneasy.

"Are you ready to get out of bed?"

"Uh huh." Nic ran her hand through her hair and sighed. She needed a shower, the hotter the better.

"Okay, so let's get your legs under you. I think a fresh gown is in order don't you?" Anne said, pulling the covers back.

She'd taken a short walk around her room in the morning and then a longer one down the hall and back. It had been more like a marathon than a sprint.

"Okay, up." Nic said, reaching for the bed rail as she swung her legs down. Her toes touched the floor, but the nurse held her back.

"Not so fast, Colonel, let me help you," the nurse said, slipping her arm under Nic as she wrapped her arm around Nic's waist and shouldered Nic up. "There you go."

Nic felt her body sway slightly and her stomach roll as she stood and then she planted her feet firm, steadying herself. *God, this isn't getting any easier,* Nic thought, gripping the rail for balance. *Where the head goes, the body follows. Stand up straight.* Pushing herself through the pain, she looked up and narrowed her focus to one thing—getting to the bathroom, taking care of herself, and determined to take a shower.

"Shower," she pushed through a clenched jaw.

"I'll talk to the doctor and see if it's on the orders. If so, we'll wrap that cast and put you in the shower."

"Thanks." Nic shuffled to the bathroom, rested on the frame, and caught sight of her reflection in the mirror. Hideous. Nic couldn't stand the sight of her right now and she wouldn't force herself on Claire, not like this.

"Do you need a hand, Colonel?"

Nic shook her head and pushed through the door. Working her way down to the toilet would take all of her energy, but it wouldn't stop her. She was determined to get back on her feet and on her way home, if it took every last ounce of her strength. She shook with the effort as her muscles strained to keep her from falling over. *Keep it together, Nic.* She wasn't going to be undone by a damn toilet.

"You okay in there, Colonel?"

"Uh huh."

Finally she hoisted herself up and shuffled to the sink to wash up. Nic couldn't avoid looking at her reflection. It made her sick, the black and blue bruises stretching into khaki and then flesh tones. Her lips weren't as swollen, but her jaw hurt like a son-of-a-bitch. The blood in the white of her eye was still as vivid and she could only imagine that her other eye looked even worse.

"You ready, Colonel?"

Nic nodded, turned, and tried to walk without shuffling. Nic tried to lengthen her stride and bend her knees more. Stretching the muscles, she felt them start to cramp due to inactivity.

"Colonel...where—"

"Out," she huffed, moving out the door and into the hallway.

"I don't think this is a good idea, Colonel." The nurse came up on Nic and slipped her arm around Nic's waist. Nic tried to push her off but almost toppled sideways. Nic shot her a look that said back off, but the nurse had been here before with bigger men than Nic and she didn't move. "Whoa there, Colonel, I'm the medical professional here. You've been in bed for a long time. Too much activity will land you right back off your feet and wishing you'd followed doctor's orders. So one thing at a time, let's get you to the shower and back in bed. I promise, we'll take you back out later. Okay?"

Nic hated it when someone was more right than she was determined. "Fine." She acquiesced, turning back around. A shower suddenly sounded perfect and then another thought struck her, Claire. She wondered what Claire was doing right now...how mad she was at her...how would she make things right between them. She sighed, how bad had she made things between them? Nic choked up and tried to swallow back the tears that threatened to spill. She needed Claire, but didn't know what to do.

"Colonel, are you okay?"

Nic wiped her eyes, gave a quick nod, and trodded back to her room. A shower would help her feel better, hopefully.

Chapter Thirty-one

Determination coursed through Claire's veins. She didn't fly half way around the world to have Nic turn her away. She didn't have any answers as to why Nic didn't want to see her, other than what the doctor had told her last night, but she would find out straight from the patient's mouth. She'd called the charge nurse at every shift change and they still didn't have any answers for her, so she was going to see Nic, and if she didn't like it, well...tough.

Claire made another stop at the coffee shop on the first floor, picked up two coffees, and looked around, expecting to see Dr. Morton. Relieved, she weaved past the crowd, dressed mostly in scrubs and lab coats, assembling for their coffee fix before reporting to work. Claire's hand shook as she punched the button for the fourth floor. She was more than a little nervous, or maybe it was anxiety, she couldn't tell, but she did know that she wasn't going to let Nic push her away. That wasn't an option, she kept telling herself.

The swish of the elevator doors opening exposed the hustle of the nurse's station straight ahead. Claire realized that early morning had a nervous energy to it. The hospital buzzed with military precision. Meals, meds, and rounds were tightly scripted around a timeline that didn't allow for mistakes. Dietary was pushing the food cart past her; the smell of breakfast foods swished past her. Nic wouldn't be eating that, but maybe she would appreciate the offering of coffee Claire brought. Slipping past the station, she ignored the nurses and doctors going over daily rounds and patient charts.

Claire weaved past a patient or two in wheelchairs pushing themselves down the hall. A patient down the hall was standing with her back to Claire, hugging an IV pole with a nurse on her elbow. She would know that tall, stretch of woman from anywhere, Nic. Slowing down, she watched as Nic pushed her IV stand down the hall. It was a slow shuffle and from her posturing, Claire could tell Nic was in pain by the way her knuckles, turning white, clenched the pole. Nic stopped and tried to straighten up and then waited for a moment before she started back down the hall. Stopping, Nic turned around and faced Claire.

Claire's heart pounded as she waited for Nic to see her. Her hands shook and the bag she had tucked under her arm almost slipped to the floor before she squeezed it closer to her body. To her right was a bathroom and she almost ducked into it. She wasn't sure why, but she suddenly didn't want Nic to see her while Nic was working so hard to get her feet under her. She knew Nic and Nic wasn't a good patient when she had a cold. She knew what it took for Nic to let the nurse help her as she tried to walk. Caught like a deer in the headlights, they both froze when her gaze locked with Nic's. Claire flinched a little when she took in all of Nic. She hadn't realized just how bad Nic was injured when Nic was laying on the bed, but now she could take in all of Nic and she felt queasy seeing the bruises, but the worst for Claire was the pain etched on Nic's face. That kind of pain that made someone seem older, frail, almost fragile. That's what hurt Claire the most. The bruises would heal and disappear, but the old Nic was gone, replaced with one Claire almost didn't recognize and she suddenly realized that was who Nic didn't want her to see, this Nic. She was sure that in Nic's mind, gone was the officer who had whisked in and saved her from the despair of loneliness.

Nic's didn't smile, she didn't frown, her face was a blank slate, no emotion at all. Claire bit her lip and tried not to cry, but her eyes welled up with tears. Swallowing hard, she walked towards Nic, who had stopped walking and only stood staring at Claire.

"Hi," she said, tentatively.

Nic's lips moved but barely anything came out.

"I brought coffee." Claire held up the cups, smiling. "I brought you some pajamas too. I thought you might like to get out of that gown. Not that it's not sexy on you, but I know it's pretty revealing. I mean, you got your parts sticking out." A nervous giggle slipped out as she pointed to Nic's knobby knees. Nic didn't laugh. "Sorry." She turned to the nurse. "Would you mind if I helped out?" Claire said, holding the coffee out to the nurse.

"I don't know." The nurse squirmed when Claire insisted that she grab the coffee.

"I think we'll be all right." Claire gave up her purse and bag to the nurse. "We'll just be right here in the hallway. Right?" She looked up at Nic and smiled. She wasn't going to be deterred, by either the nurse or Nic.

"Here, let me help you." Claire avoided looking at Nic and grabbed the assist strap around Nic's hips the nurse had been holding on to. "Ready?"

Without much effort, Claire slowly walked with Nic down the hall, nothing said between them. They stopped, shifted around, and headed back down the hall towards Nic's room.

"I've missed you," Claire said, rubbing her face against the thin robe. "You smell good."

"Shower," Nic said, without looking at Claire.

"Would you like some coffee?"

Nic nodded and Claire turned them towards Nic's room. She could hear Nic grunt with each step and then stopped. Clearly Nic was tired and it was taking more effort for her to move. Sweat beaded up on Nic's forehead and her breathing became more labored, scaring Claire.

"Want me to get a wheelchair?"

Nic finally looked at her, shaking her head. "No," she hissed.

"Okay, let's get you to bed."

Claire guided Nic to the edge of the bed, clean sheets tucked tightly at the corners; an edge peeled back waited for her. Nic turned around and faced Claire, leaning against the bed.

"Here, hold on to my shoulder and I'll help you get in to bed." She grabbed Nic's middle and Nic groaned in pain. "Oh shit, sorry...I didn't mean to..."

"Fine," Nic said, sitting down on the edge of the bed.

As Nic moved to lift her legs, Claire stopped her. "Wait, do you want to change into the pjs I brought?" Claire looked at Nic, hopeful. "At least the bottoms?" She pulled the flannel jammies out of the bag. "They're men's...the shirt buttons, so I thought that would be easier to get on and off...with your injuries and all."

Claire slipped down to her knees, slipped a leg

of the flannel pajamas on each of Nic's legs, and slid them up to where she rested against the bed. Standing, she put Nic's hand on her shoulder and waited. "Here, let me pull this and I can bring you forward off the bed," she said, grabbing the assist strap still around Nic's waist.

In unison, they moved closer and Claire slipped the flannel pants up over Nic's hips. She could feel Nic's breath on her face, so she looked up and kissed Nic on the cheek. "I love you," she whispered.

They stood silent for a moment. Claire didn't want to move away, afraid that it might be a while before they were this close again. "Please don't make me leave, Nic. I don't want to be anywhere else but right here with you."

Nic pushed Claire slightly as she sat back down and tried to bring her legs up on bed. Looking away from Claire, she slipped off the robe and pulled at the ties behind her neck, yanking off the hospital gown.

Claire gasped at the road map of cuts and bruises on Nic's torso. Her body was wrapped tight with a bandage for her broken ribs, but bruises peeked out above and below the bandages and extended down under her flannel pants. Claire hadn't notice them when she slipped the pants on, but now she couldn't help but see them. The side of Nic's right breast was swollen and bruised. There was little skin on Nic's right side that wasn't affected.

She reached out to touch Nic, but Nic flinched away. "I'm sorry, I didn't mean to react that way. Here, let me help you get the top on," Claire said, grabbing the top and unbuttoning it. "Nic?" Tears streamed down Nic's face and she still didn't look at Claire.

"Nic." Claire walked to the other side of the bed

and stood in front of Nic. "Stop it. I don't care how you look, I love you, and I'm not going to leave you," Claire said as she too started to cry. "I'm sorry baby, I didn't expect you to be so bad...I mean I..." Claire grabbed Nic's hand, brought it to her lips, and kissed her palm. She hadn't prepared herself for the damage done to Nic's body. Her only thought was one of thankfulness that Nic was alive.

Nic tried to pull her hand away, but Claire held it. "I'm not going to let you shut me out, Nic. It's bad, so what. We'll get through it. That's what couples do, Nic. Remember, in sickness and health. Would you leave me here alone?" She stared at Nic, waiting for a response. "Would you?"

Nic's lip quivered as she shook her head. She still wouldn't look at Claire, but she knew Nic could hear her, so Claire pressed on.

"You can make me leave, but I'm not going anywhere. You might see a monster when you look in the mirror, but I see the love of my life in front of me. I see the woman who survived a helicopter crash in Iraq, I see the woman who brought Mike home when she didn't have to, I see the woman who makes me feel things I've never felt before. That I didn't think I'd ever feel." Claire kissed Nic's palm again and then pressed Nic's hand against her cheek. Choking back tears, her voice cracked as she continued. "My life wouldn't be complete without you in it, Nic. It would be empty, hollow, and what about Grace...what would she do without her Nickie?"

Claire's heart was breaking for her lover. She cried harder as she thought about Nic alone, without the support of family and friends to get through this.

"I wasn't there when you were wounded before,

but I'm here now, so why would you take that away from us?" Suddenly Claire's voice was laced with a hint of anger. "Why would you push me away, Nic? I thought you loved me?"

Nic pulled her hand away and grabbed at the pen and paper. Scribbling, she handed Claire the paper.

"Look at me," Claire read the scrawl. Her chest hurt; the pain sliced right through her. It was all about how Nic looked. "So...you're worried that I find you... what...a monster?"

Nic closed her eyes, tears squeezing past their barrier. She turned her head away from Claire and sucked in a ragged breath. Claire started to reached for Nic's face, she wanted to touch her, but she stopped. Standing, she grabbed the flannel shirt.

"Sit up, Nic. You need to put this on," Claire said flatly.

Nic raised up and slid her left arm into the sleeve. Claire pushed a lock of hair behind Nic's ear and let her fingers linger, following the curve of it before she pushed the shirt across Nic's back and walked around to the other side to button it closed. She covered Nic's arm, not wanting to look at the bruises and cuts that were the source of Nic's discomfort.

"Knock, knock. Colonel Caldwell, are you awake?" Dr. Morton walked in tentatively, peeking around the curtain. "Mrs. Caldwell, it's good to see you again. How are you?"

Claire wiped at her eyes before shaking Dr. Morton's hand. "Good, thank you."

"Colonel, I hear you were doing laps around the ward today?"

Nic pulled a tissue and wiped her nose, then nodded.

"Well, I stopped by because I wanted to look at your eye and see how it's healing."

Dr. Morton walked to the other side of the bed and pulled a pair of scissors. Ringing the nurse's station, he called for a nurse to attend the unveiling.

"Well, let's see what our handy work looks like, Colonel. Are you ready?"

Nic shrugged and then looked towards Claire. She offered a slight smile of reassurance and then took the chair next to the bed to watch. A nurse with a small tote full of bandages, tape, and other medical item entered the room. "Good morning, Dr. Morton. How are you today?"

"Good, Michelle. I'm going to take the Colonel's bandages off and check out her eye. Once I'm finished, would you rewrap, please?"

"Of course," she said, setting the tote on the bed, slipping on pair of latex gloves.

"Okay, Colonel, I want you to keep your eye closed after I've removed the bandages. We'll turn the lights off and then you can slowly open your eyes. Don't expect great things. With the amount of damage that was done, we'll be lucky if you have partial sight."

Claire suddenly wanted to pull him aside and have words with the doctor. What kind of crap what this? Didn't he see how fragile Nic was? She didn't need to have her hopes dashed. She needed to be… to be…what…what was she thinking, her head was spinning. Her thoughts were all over the place as she watched the doctor slide the scissors along Nic's temple, cutting the bandages away. What would Nic do if she couldn't see? If she thought she was damaged goods before, this would only push her over the edge she was dangling from.

The scissors snipped through the first layer of bandages with ease, allowing the doctor to unwrap the last layer from Nic's head. The bruising was worse than Claire expected to see as he pulled the pad from Nic's eye. Nic's eyelid and the skin under her eye was black, bluing at the edges. A crisp red line bisected the bruising. Claire suspected this was from the surgery. The white of Nic's eye was blood red, almost matching the left eye, which had started to fade to a lighter shade of pink. Swallowing hard, Claire took a deep breath; she suddenly felt a cold sweat sweep over her entire body. Wiping at the sweat on her forehead, she leaned back and continued to take slow deep breaths. *Don't faint,* she told herself.

"Mrs. Caldwell, are you all right?"

Claire looked over at the nurse and found everyone looking at her. *Oh Christ!*

"I'm fine."

Nic turned towards Claire and grimaced.

"I'm fine, really." Claire stood and walked over to the bed, rubbing Nic's shoulder.

"So Colonel, this might hurt a bit," he said as he popped on a pen light and looked in Nic's eye.

Nic flinched as the light waved back and forth across.

"Can you follow my finger?" He waved his finger in front of her face. "How many of my fingers do you see?"

Nic's eyes tracked the finger as it moved back and forth in front of her face. Claire sighed, relieved to see Nic's eyes following the doctor. Then Nic held up two fingers and Claire's heart sunk.

"Well, Colonel, that's to be expected. It'll take about a week to two weeks for the double vision to go away, but it looks good. You don't have any eye drooping, so it looks like we were able to stabilize the fracture. Remember, don't blow your nose, keep ice on the swelling and it should start to go down. We'll keep the lights dim until you're more comfortable with light. I have to say you're a lucky person, Colonel." Dr. Morton tucked his pen in his pocket and turned towards Claire. "We'll probably transport her to Walter Reed within the week, assuming she continues to improve."

"Thank you, doctor."

"My pleasure." Dr. Morton turned back to Nic. "Don't push yourself, Colonel. Life will still be waiting, and so will the Corps."

Nic nodded and extended her left hand. "Tanks, doc."

"You bet, Colonel. I love it when we can send one home with all their parts intact."

"Wait," Nic said. Pointing to her jaw, she said, "How long?"

"Aw, well I'd say you have another five to six weeks. I know that's a long time, but I'll make sure dietary stops by and gets you set up on a special diet. It isn't uncommon for someone who's had their jaw wired shut to lose some weight, but a good plan can help you. You'll probably be on a liquid diet or soft diet for at least the next two months. Don't worry, once you've got the wires out, you'll put the weight back on."

"'Kay," Nic said, nodding.

"Take care of yourself." Doctor Morton shook Nic's hand and then patted Claire on the shoulder. "Take care of her, Mrs. Caldwell."

"I plan on it. Thank you, Doctor Morton," Claire

said, looking at Nic while she shook the doctor's hand. "I plan on it."

Suddenly Claire and Nic were alone in the room, the lights dimmed and Nic's prognosis good. Claire slid her hip on the bed, facing Nic. She studied her wife's face. Nothing could change the way she felt about Nic, no matter what she looked like. Now she needed to convince her wife of that fact. Claire ran her finger along Nic's hand, following the veins with her finger. Looking up, she smiled and scooted closer to Nic.

"I love you. I'll love you forever and a scar here or there isn't going to change that. Let me make this as clear as I possibly can, there is nothing you can do to make me stop loving you, so quit trying, you're just wasting your time."

Claire pulled Nic's wedding ring out of her pocket. Holding it between her fingers, she pulled Nic's hand up and slid it on. "I'd marry you all over again, baby. Besides, you promised me a wedding when you got back from Afghanistan and I'm going to hold you to that promise, do you understand?"

Nic looked down at the ring and then up at Claire.

"We'll make this work, Honey. I'm not going anywhere, not without you." Claire leaned in and placed a soft kiss on Nic's lips. "I know your recovery isn't going to be easy, but you don't have to do it alone." Claire raised Nic's hand to her lips and placed a soft kiss on her knuckles. "Let's go home, I know a little girl who wants to see her Nickie."

Epilogue

Nic sat in the sun, soaking up all she could before she had to leave for her doctor's appointment. The wall of windows in the small house had the best view of the forest below. Claire had surprised her when she returned from Walter Reed. Nic couldn't blame Claire for wanting a house. Truth be told, it would probably have been months before Nic could even wrap her head around the process of looking at houses, let alone purchase one. She had to admit that the house gave her a sense of stability, somewhere, something she knew couldn't be taken away from them.

She watched as the fingers of fog threatened to devour another house as it crept closer inland. She loved sitting here, alone, watching the world outside. She rested her head against the wingback and watched. She couldn't close her eyes. Every time she did, she went to a place she'd rather forget, a ditch in Afghanistan. The nightmares were finally getting fewer and further between. She rubbed her jaw; the phantom pain lingered, especially when she awoke from a nightmare.

She'd taken to sleeping in a separate room. Her thrashing around had hurt Claire on more than one occasion and it wounded Nic to see her wife hurt at her own hand, even if she couldn't control it. Besides, Claire needed her sleep now that she was back in school and separate rooms had been the only solution. Claire hated it and often times Nic would find her curled up next to her in the middle of the night. So much for keeping Claire out of harm's way.

They'd decided to wait on the wedding until Nic's scars were healed. It was a small concession Claire had made for Nic's dignity, but Nic knew the internal scars would never heal.

She'd been alone with her thoughts, and her memories, and Nic could barely cope. A wired jaw and the post-surgical bruising of her last surgery kept her from going out. So she sequestered herself in the new home Claire had surprised her with when she got home from Walter Reed. She didn't have the energy to be mad; on the scale of problems, this was a first world problem that in the bigger scheme of things was nothing.

Buzz, buzz, buzz. Nic's phone vibrated. Looking down, she didn't recognize the number. Her finger hovered over the end button, but for some reason she answered it instead.

"Colonel Caldwell?"

"Yes, who's this?" The voice had a ring of familiarity, but she couldn't place it.

"Sgt. Ramirez, ma'am."

Nic had finally seen Ramirez at the hospital in Germany, literally just minutes before Ramirez was leaving for the states. While the conversation had been brief, more note passing than actual words, Nic had been able to convey her regret over the whole situation. They shared phone numbers and promised to keep in contact, but as usually happens, Nic suspected they wouldn't. Distance and time had a way of pushing people apart, rather than bring them together.

"Ramirez, how are you?"

"Ma'am, I'm good. I just thought I'd check in on you and see how you're doing. I waited a few weeks until I thought you had your wires taken out."

"Yeah, I got them out a week ago, still on soft foods."

"Well, that's good, right? I mean no more scribbling on note pads."

"Even better, I have my cast off and can write legibly now. So how are you?"

"I'm still on a medical profile, waiting to be clear for duty, but I'm good. Being home has allowed me to spend time with my daughter and family."

"That's great."

"Yeah, my mom and abuela are constantly hovering over me, so I'll be ready to get back to work."

"Overseas?"

"Naw, I think I'm requesting duty stateside. Two injuries is my limit. Besides, I've wanted to make some changes in my life."

"Anything I can help with?" Nic said.

When you spend extended periods of time living in a Humvee with someone, you get to a point where you learn a lot about that person, and Nic liked Ramirez. She understood her silence *and* her anger and they'd taken a liking to each other. A battle buddy was your family overseas and now she considered Ramirez part of her family, too.

"Naw, I got this, but thanks. How about you, what are you going to do now?"

Nic had thought about that a lot lately. Would she stay and finish out her time to retirement? It was only a few years, but God only knew what the Marine Corps had for her this time. She was still on a medical profile and in fact was being assessed today to find out if she could report back to duty or if they medically retired her. Her research position had been approved at NPS, so if she wanted it, she could do what she originally planned, but that would mean she would have to stay on active status and now she wasn't so sure she wanted that.

She'd be on a permanent profile physically and that ate at her. She would always be *less-than* in her mind. Less-than able to meet the Marine Corps standards.

"I'm not sure yet. Two injuries might be my limit as well. Besides, Claire isn't too crazy about the possibility of me being shipped out again."

"I hear ya. I'm not too crazy about the thought of being shipped out again either, that's why I'm changing my MOS to something else. Being a gunner was a rush, but I think it's time to get some skills I can use in the real world." Ramirez chuckled softly. "Don't know what those skills are, but I'll figure it out."

"I know you will, Sergeant, you're tough and resilient, I can't think of a company that wouldn't be happy to have someone like you working for them."

"Thanks, Colonel."

"So, you're down in L.A.?"

"Yes, ma'am."

"Why don't you and your daughter come up for a visit? We have a little play buddy for your daughter and it would be great to touch base again."

"Uh, I don't know, ma'am…"

Nic knew Ramirez's hesitation. Nic an officer, Ramirez an enlisted; it was hard to break those lines of fraternization once they had been drilled into your head for so long.

"Ramirez, we aren't on the battlefield anymore, I'm not your boss and who knows, after today I might not be in anymore. What do you say? I'd like to think we can move beyond the battle lines and be friends, but hey, I don't want to pressure you or remind you I did save your life," Nic said, a hint of lightness in her voice.

"Is that an order, ma'am?"

"No." Nic laughed. "Just hoping you'll take some time off and hang out with a friend."

"How about I see what I can do, I'm not making any promises, but when would this little trek take place?"

"How about the Thanksgiving break? That way you have two weeks to think about it and let me know."

"Will do, Colonel. Well, I better let you go, I need to fix lunch for my Carolina."

"You got it and hey, I just want to thank you for everything you did over in Afghanistan. I appreciate you having my six."

Nic was glad Ramirez had her back.

"Hey, you're the one who had my six. If it wasn't for you, I wouldn't be here."

"Just doin' my job." Nic shifted the subject before they went somewhere she wasn't ready to explore yet. "Hey, let me know about Thanksgiving."

"Roger that, Colonel."

"Sounds good and maybe by the time you get up here you can call me Nic."

"Highly unlikely, Colonel."

"Well, work on it and I'll see you in two weeks."

Without confirmation, Ramirez just said, "Talk to you soon. My best to your wife."

"Thanks, take care."

With that, Ramirez was off and Nic was ready for her appointment. Nic turned when she heard the front door open and was surprised when Claire walked through.

"What are you doing home?"

"Well, I wanted to be with you when you went to the doctor's today."

Claire hadn't missed an appointment yet, even though Nic had told her she was more than capable of driving herself. It had become a ritual of sorts, doctor's office, lunch, and then a walk on the beach to talk about what Nic's future looked like. Oh, they talked about other stuff, but never what happened over in Afghanistan. Nic knew Claire was waiting for her to unload, but right now, she just couldn't. It was too fresh; the pain and her injuries were like a tattoo laid at the surface for everyone to see, and she would never be rid of it. So she would just have to adjust to seeing it every day. Her face was almost back to normal, her missing teeth replaced with implants, her wrist and ribs had healed, and every now and then she had a spell of double vision. But the memories of that day, those were etched, a mental scar she would never get rid of.

"So, did you do anything exciting this morning?" Claire wrapped her arms around Nic's waist and cradled her head against Nic's chest. Instinctively, Nic turned and kissed the top of Claire's head, the smell of spearmint lingering around her. She was so glad to be home.

"Nope, got Grace off to school, made my bed–"

"When are you going to move back into the bedroom with me?"

"Soon." Was all Nic could say.

"Anything else?"

"I got a call from Ramirez just now."

Claire pulled back and looked at Nic. "She okay?"

"She's fine. I invited her to Thanksgiving." Nic hadn't discussed it with Claire, but if she knew Claire....

"Did she say yes?"

"Not exactly, but I have a good feeling."

Claire snuggled back against Nic. "I hope she can make it."

"Me too."

"Well, are you ready for today?"

"Ready as I'm ever going to be," Nic said, kissing Claire's head. Nic pulled off and grabbed her medical file. This was a new doctor who would decide Nic's fate, so she needed all of her records for a complete profile. "Let's go."

Claire pulled Nic's arm, stopping her from leaving. She grabbed Nic's hand, raised it to her lips, and then said, "I want you to know that no matter what happens today, I love you and I'm all in." Rising up on her toes, she wrapped her arms around Nic's neck and slowly, sensually kissed her. Nic kissed Claire back and felt that familiar tingle surge through her body, the first signs she had since returning that life was getting back to normal, sort of.

"I love you and I don't think you know how thankful I am to have you in my life."

Nic kissed Claire again, ran a hand down Claire's hip, and waited a moment; when Claire intensified the kiss, she reached around, cupped her ass, and pulled Claire closer.

"Forever, my lover, I'm forever faithful to you," Nic said, resting her head against Claire's.

Coming in 2015 - Faithful Valor

Nic and Claire have survived a deployment to Afghanistan. However, can they survive what's coming next? Stay tuned for *Faithful Valor* as Nic and Claire's love is tested when a fellow student presses all the right buttons while Nic is gone, yet again.

About the Author

Isabella lives on the central coast with her wife, and three sons. She teaches college and in her spare time, which there seems to be little of lately. She is working on her writers retreat in the Sierra foothills for those that want a quieter place to learn and work. She is a GCLS award winner for, Always Faithful and a finalist for Scarlet Masquerade. She also finaled in the International National Book awards and has two honorable mentions in the Rainbow Awards.

She also writes under the nom de plume - Jett Abbott. A darker, rogue who's a motorcycle enthusiast and loves people watching.

Like her fan page for the latest in news on readings, appearances and books.

https://www.facebook.com/isabella.sapphirebooks
or
www.sapphirebooks.com/isabella.html

Other Isabella titles available at Sapphire Books

Award winning novel - Always Faithful
ISBN - 978-0-9828608-0-9

Major Nichol "Nic" Caldwell is the only survivor of her helicopter crash in Iraq. She is left alone to wonder why she and she alone. Survivor's guilt has nothing on the young Major as she is forced to deal with the scars, both physical and mental, left from her ordeal overseas. Before the accident, she couldn't think of doing anything else in her life.

Claire Monroe is your average military wife, with a loving husband and a little girl. She is used to the time apart from her husband. In fact, it was one of the reasons she married him. Then, one day, her life is turned upside down when she gets a visit from the Marine Corps.

Can these two women come to terms with the past and finally find happiness, or will their shared sense of honor keep them apart?

Broken Shield
ISBN - 978-0-9828608-2-3

Tyler Jackson, former paramedic now firefighter, has seen her share of death up close. The death of her wife caused Tyler to rethink her career choices, but the death of her mother two weeks later cemented her return to the ranks of firefighter. Her path of self-destruction and womanizing is just a front to hide the heartbreak and devastation she lives with every day. Tyler's given up on finding love and having the family she's always wanted. When tragedy strikes her life for a second time she finds something she thought she lost.

Ashley Henderson loves her job. Ignoring her mother's advice, she opts for a career in law enforcement. But, Ashley hides a secret that soon turns her life upside down. Shame, guilt and fear keep Ashley from venturing forward and finding the love she so desperately craves. Her life comes crashing down around her in one swift moment forcing her to come clean about her secrets and her life.

Can two women thrust together by one traumatic event survive and find love together, or will their past force them apart?

American Yakuza
ISBN - 978-0-9828608-3-0

Luce Potter straddles three cultures as she strives to live with the ideals of family, honor, and duty. When her grandfather passes the family business to her, Luce finds out that power, responsibility and justice come with a price. Is it a price she's willing to die for?
Brooke Erickson lives the fast-paced life of an investigative journalist living on the edge until it all comes crashing down around her one night in Europe. Stateside, Brooke learns to deal with a new reality when she goes to work at a financial magazine and finds out things aren't always as they seem.

Can two women find enough common ground for love or will their two different worlds and cultures keep them apart?

Executive Disclosure
ISBN - 978-0-9828608-3-0

When a life is threatened, it takes a special breed of person to step in front of a bullet. Chad Morgan's job has put her life on the line more times that she can count. Getting close to the client is expected; getting too close could be deadly for Chad. Reagan Reynolds wants the top job at Reynolds Holdings and knows how to play the game like "the boys". She's not above using her beauty and body as currency to get what she wants. Shocked to find out someone wants her dead, Reagan isn't thrilled at the prospect of needing protection as she tries to convince the board she's the right woman for a man's job. How far will a killer go to get what they want? Secrets and deception twist the rules of the game as a killer closes in. How far will Chad go to protect her beautiful, but challenging client?

American Yakuza II - The Lies that Bind
ISBN - 978-10939062-20-8

Luce Potter runs her life and her business with an iron fist and complete control until lies and deception unravel her world. The shadow of betrayal consumes Luce, threatening to destroy the most precious thing in her life, Brooke Erickson.

Brooke Erickson finds herself on the outside of Luce's life looking in. As events spiral out of control Brooke can only watch as the woman she loves pushes her further away. Suddenly, devastated and alone, Brooke refuses to let go without an explanation.

Colby Water, a federal agent investigating the ever-elusive Luce Potter, discovers someone from her past is front and center in her investigation of the Yakuza crime leader. Before she can put the crime boss in prison, she must confront the ultimate deception in her professional life.

When worlds collide, betrayal, dishonor and death are inevitable. Can Luce and Brooke survive the explosion?

Surviving Reagan
ISBN - 978-1-939062-38-3

Chad Morgan has finally worked through the betrayal of her former client and lover, Reagan Reynolds. Putting the pieces of her life back in order, she finds herself on a collision course with that past when she takes on a new client, the future first lady. Unfortunately, Chad's newest job puts her in the cross-hairs of a domestic terrorist determined to release a virus that could kill thousands of women.

Reagan Reynolds has paid for her sins and is ready to start a new life. Attending a business conference in Abu Dhabi gives her the opportunity to prove to her father and herself that she's worthy of a fresh start. Her past will intersect with her future at the conference when she accidentally comes face-to-face with Chad Morgan.

Time is running out. Will Reagan confront Chad? Can she convince Chad she's changed, or will death part them forever?

Writing as Jett Abbott

Writing as Jett Abbott

Scarlet Masquerade
ISBN - 978-0-982860-81-6

What do you say to the woman you thought died over a century ago? Will time heal all wounds or does it just allow them to fester and grow? A.J. Locke has lived over two centuries and works like a demon, both figuratively and literally. As the owner of a successful pharmaceutical company that specializes in blood research, she has changed the way she can live her life. Wanting for nothing, she has smartly compartmentalized her life so that when she needs to, she can pick up and start all over again, which happens every twenty years or so. Love is not an emotion A.J. spends much time on. Since losing the love of her life to the plague one hundred fifty years ago, she vowed to never travel down that road again. That isn't to say she doesn't have women when she wants them, she just wants them on her terms and that doesn't involve a long term commitment.

A.J.'s cool veneer is peeled back when she sees the love of her life in a lesbian bar, in the same town, in the same day and time in which she lives. Is her mind playing tricks on her? If not, how did Clarissa survive the plague when she had made A.J. promise never to change her?

Clarissa Graham is a university professor who has lived an obscure life teaching English literature. She has made it a point to stay off the radar and never become involved with anything that resembles her past life. Every once in a while Clarissa has an itch that needs to be scratched, so she finds an out of the way location to scratch it. She keeps her personal life separate from her professional one, and in doing so she is able to keep her secrets to herself. Suddenly, her life is turned upside down when someone tries to kill her. She finds herself in the middle of an assassination plot with no idea who wants her dead

Scarlet Assassin
ISBN 978-1-939062-36-9

Selene Hightower is a killer for hire. A vampire who walks in both the light and the darkness, but lately darkness has a stronger pull. Her unfinished business could cost her the ability to live in the light, throwing her permanently back into the black ink of evil.

Doctor Francesca Swartz led a boring life filled with test tubes, blood trials, and work. One exploratory night, in a world of leather and torture, she is intrigued by a dark and solitary soul. She surrenders to temptation and the desire to experience something new, only to discover that it might alter her life forever.

Will Selene allow the light to win over the darkness threatening the edges of her life? Two women wonder if they can co-exist despite vast differences, as worlds collide and threaten to destroy any hope of happiness. Who will win?

CPSIA information can be obtained
at www.ICGtesting.com
Printed in the USA
LVOW08s1954260517
535804LV00001B/22/P